DAMON
RUNYON

THE SNATCHING OF BOOKIE BOB AND OTHER STORIES

D1324835

PENGUIN BOOKS

PENGUIN BOOKS

Published by the Penguin Group. Penguin Books Ltd, 27 Wrights Lane, London w8 5TZ, England. Penguin Books USA Inc., 375 Hudson Street, New York, New York 10014, USA. Penguin Books Australia Ltd, Ringwood, Victoria, Australia. Penguin Books Canada Ltd, 10 Alcorn Avenue, Toronto, Ontario, Canada M4V 3B2. Penguin Books (NZ) Ltd, 182–190 Wairau Road, Auckland 10, New Zealand · Penguin Books Ltd, Registered Offices: Harmondsworth, Middlesex, England · **These stories are taken from *On Broadway*, published by Penguin Books in 1990.** This edition published 1995 · Copyright 1950–1975 by the Estate of the late Damon Runyon. All rights reserved · Typeset by Datix International Limited, Bungay, Suffolk. Printed in England by Clays Ltd, St Ives plc · Except in the United States of America, this book is sold subject to the condition that it shall not, by way of trade or otherwise, be lent, re-sold, hired out, or otherwise circulated without the publisher's prior consent in any form of binding or cover other than that in which it is published and without a similar condition including this condition being imposed on the subsequent purchaser · 10 9 8 7 6 5 4 3 2 1

CONTENTS

The Snatching of Bookie Bob

Now it comes on the spring of 1931, after a long hard winter, and times are very tough indeed, what with the stock market going all to pieces, and banks busting right and left, and the law getting very nasty about this and that, and one thing and another, and many citizens of this town are compelled to do the best they can.

There is very little scratch anywhere and along Broadway many citizens are wearing their last year's clothes and have practically nothing to bet on the races or anything else, and it is a condition that will touch anybody's heart.

So I am not surprised to hear rumours that the snatching of certain parties is going on in spots, because while snatching is by no means a high-class business, and is even considered somewhat illegal, it is something to tide over the hard times.

Furthermore, I am not surprised to hear that this snatching is being done by a character by the name of Harry the Horse, who comes from Brooklyn, and who is a character who does not care much what sort of business he is in, and who is mobbed up with other characters from Brooklyn such as Spanish John and Little Isadore, who do not care what sort of business they are in, either.

In fact, Harry the Horse and Spanish John and Little Isadore are very hard characters in every respect, and there is considerable indignation expressed around and about when they move over from Brooklyn into Manhattan and start snatching, because the citizens of Manhattan feel that if there is any snatching done in their territory, they are entitled to do it themselves.

But Harry the Horse and Spanish John and Little Isadore pay no attention whatever to local sentiment and go on the snatch on a pretty fair scale, and by and by I am hearing rumours of some very nice scores. These scores are not extra large scores, to be sure, but they are enough to keep the wolf from the door, and in fact from three different doors, and before long Harry the Horse and Spanish John and Little Isadore are around the race-tracks betting on the horses, because if there is one thing they are all very fond of, it is betting on the horses.

Now many citizens have the wrong idea entirely of the snatching business. Many citizens think that all there is to snatching is to round up the party who is to be snatched and then just snatch him, putting him away somewhere until his family or friends dig up enough scratch to pay whatever price the snatchers are asking. Very few citizens understand that the snatching business must be well organized and very systematic.

In the first place, if you are going to do any snatching, you cannot snatch just anybody. You must know who you are snatching, because naturally it is no good snatching somebody who does not have any scratch to settle with. And you cannot tell by the way a party looks or how he lives in this town if he has any scratch, because many a party who is around in automobiles, and wearing good clothes, and chucking quite a swell is nothing but the phonus bolonus and does not have any real scratch whatever.

So of course such a party is no good for snatching, and of course guys who are on the snatch cannot go around inquiring into bank accounts, or asking how much this and that party has in a safe-deposit vault, because such questions are apt to make citizens wonder why, and it is very dangerous to get citizens to wondering why about anything. So the only way guys who are on the snatch can find out about parties worth snatching is to make a connection with some guy who can put the finger on the right party.

The finger guy must know the party he fingers has plenty of ready scratch to begin with, and he must also know that this party is such a party as is not apt to make too much disturbance about being snatched, such as telling the gendarmes. The party may be a legitimate party, such as a business guy, but he will have reasons why he does not wish it to get out that he is snatched, and the finger must know these reasons. Maybe the party is not leading the right sort of life, such as running around with blondes when he has an ever-loving wife and seven children in Mamaroneck, but does not care to have his habits known, as is apt to happen if he is snatched, especially if he is snatched when he is with a blonde.

And sometimes the party is such a party as does not care to have matches run up and down the bottom of his feet, which often happens to parties who are snatched and who do not seem to wish to settle their bill promptly, because many parties are very ticklish on the bottom of the feet, especially 3 if the matches are lit. On the other hand maybe the party is not a legitimate guy, such as a party who is running a crap game or a swell speakeasy, or who has some other dodge he does not care to have come out, and who also does not care about having his feet tickled.

Such a party is very good indeed for the snatching business, because he is pretty apt to settle without any argument. And after a party settles one snatching, it will be considered very unethical for anybody else to snatch him again very soon, so he is not likely to make any fuss about the matter. The finger guy gets a commission of twenty-five per cent. of the settlement, and one and all are satisfied and much fresh scratch comes into circulation, which is very good for the merchants. And while the party who is snatched may know who snatches him, one thing he never knows is who puts the finger on him, this being considered a trade secret.

I am talking to Waldo Winchester, the newspaper scribe, one night and something about the snatching business comes up, and Waldo Winchester is trying to tell me that it is one of the oldest dodges in the world, only Waldo calls it kidnapping, which is a title that will be very repulsive to guys who are on the snatch nowadays. Waldo Winchester claims that hundreds of years ago guys are around snatching parties, male and female, and holding them for ransom, and furthermore Waldo Winchester says they even snatch very little children and Waldo states that it is all a very, very wicked proposition.

Well, I can see where Waldo is right about it being wicked to snatch dolls and little children, but of course no guys who are on the snatch nowadays will ever think of such a thing, because who is going to settle for a doll in these times when you can scarcely even give them away? As for little children, they are apt to be a great nuisance, because their mammas are sure to go running around hollering bloody murder about them, and furthermore little children are very dangerous, indeed, what with being apt to break out with measles and mumps and one thing and another any minute and give it to everybody in the neighbourhood.

Well, anyway, knowing that Harry the Horse and Spanish John and Little Isadore are now on the snatch, I am by no means pleased to see them come along one Tuesday evening when I am standing at the corner of Fiftieth and Broadway, although of course I give them a very jolly hello, and say I hope and trust they are feeling nicely.

They stand there talking to me a few minutes, and I am very glad indeed that Johnny Brannigan, the strong-arm cop, does not happen along and see us, because it will give Johnny a very bad impression of me to see me in such company, even though I am not responsible for the company. But naturally I cannot haul off and walk away from this company at once, because Harry the Horse and Spanish John and Little Isadore may get the idea that I am playing the chill for them, and will feel hurt.

'Well,' I say to Harry the Horse, 'how are things going, Harry?'

'They are going no good,' Harry says. 'We do not beat a race in four days. In fact,' he says, 'we go overboard to-day. We are washed out. We owe every bookmaker at the track that will trust us, and now we are out trying to raise some 5 scratch to pay off. A guy must pay his bookmaker no matter what.'

Well, of course this is very true, indeed, because if a guy does not pay his bookmaker it will lower his business standing quite some, as the bookmaker is sure to go around putting the blast on him, so I am pleased to hear Harry the Horse mention such honourable principles.

'By the way,' Harry says, 'do you know a guy by the name of Bookie Bob?'

Now I do not know Bookie Bob personally, but of course I know who Bookie Bob is, and so does everybody else in this town that ever goes to a race-track, because Bookie Bob is the biggest bookmaker around and about, and has plenty of scratch. Furthermore, it is the opinion of one and all that Bookie Bob will die with this scratch, because he is considered a very close guy with his scratch. In fact, Bookie Bob is considered closer than a dead heat.

He is a short fat guy with a bald head, and his head is always shaking a little from side to side, which some say is a touch of palsy, but which most citizens believe comes of Bookie Bob shaking his head 'No' to guys asking for credit in betting on the races. He has an ever-loving wife, who is a very quiet little old doll with grey hair and a very sad look in her eyes, but nobody can blame her for this when they figure that she lives with Bookie Bob for many years.

I often see Bookie Bob and his ever-loving wife eating in different joints along in the Forties, because they seem to have no home except an hotel, and many a time I hear
Bookie Bob giving her a going over about something or

other, and generally it is about the price of something she orders to eat, so I judge Bookie Bob is as tough with his ever-loving wife about scratch as he is with everybody else. In fact, I hear him bawling her out one night because she has on a new hat which she says cost her six bucks, and Bookie Bob wishes to know if she is trying to ruin him with her extravagances.

But of course I am not criticizing Bookie Bob for squawking about the hat, because for all I know six bucks may be too much for a doll to pay for a hat, at that. And furthermore, maybe Bookie Bob has the right idea about keeping down his ever-loving wife's appetite, because I know many a guy in this town who is practically ruined by dolls eating too much on him.

'Well,' I say to Harry the Horse, 'if Bookie Bob is one of the bookmakers you owe, I am greatly surprised to see that you seem to have both eyes in your head, because I never before hear of Bookie Bob letting anybody owe him without giving him at least one of their eyes for security. In fact,' I say, 'Bookie Bob is such a guy as will not give you the right time if he has two watches.'

'No,' Harry the Horse says, 'we do not owe Bookie Bob. But,' he says, 'he will be owing us before long. We are going to put the snatch on Bookie Bob.'

Well, this is most disquieting news to me, not because I care if they snatch Bookie Bob or not, but because somebody may see me talking to them who will remember about it when Bookie Bob is snatched. But of course it will not be good policy for me to show Harry the Horse and Spanish

John and Little Isadore that I am nervous, so I only speak as follows:

'Harry,' I say, 'every man knows his own business best, and I judge you know what you are doing. But,' I say, 'you are snatching a hard guy when you snatch Bookie Bob. A very hard guy, indeed. In fact,' I say, 'I hear the softest thing about him is his front teeth, so it may be very difficult for you to get him to settle after you snatch him.'

'No,' Harry the Horse says, 'we will have no trouble about it. Our finger gives us Bookie Bob's hole card, and it is a most surprising thing, indeed. But,' Harry the Horse says, 'you come upon many surprising things in human nature when you are on the snatch. Bookie Bob's hole card is his ever-loving wife's opinion of him.

'You see,' Harry the Horse says, 'Bookie Bob has been putting himself away with his ever-loving wife for years as a very important guy in this town, with much power and influence, although of course Bookie Bob knows very well he stands about as good as a broken leg. In fact,' Harry the Horse says, 'Bookie Bob figures that his ever-loving wife is the only one in the world who looks on him as a big guy, and he will sacrifice even his scratch, or anyway some of it, rather than let her know that guys have such little respect for him as to put the snatch on him. It is what you call psychology,' Harry the Horse says.

Well, this does not make good sense to me, and I am thinking to myself that the psychology that Harry the Horse really figures to work out nice on Bookie Bob is tickling his feet with matches, but I am not anxious to stand there arguing about it, and pretty soon I bid them all good evening, very polite, and take the wind, and I do not see Harry the Horse or Spanish John or Little Isadore again for a month.

In the meantime, I hear gossip here and there that Bookie Bob is missing for several days, and when he finally shows up again he gives it out that he is very sick during his absence, but I can put two and two together as well as anybody in this town and I figure that Bookie Bob is snatched by Harry the Horse and Spanish John and Little Isadore, and the chances are it costs him plenty.

So I am looking for Harry the Horse and Spanish John and Little Isadore to be around the race-track with plenty of scratch and betting them higher than a cat's back, but they never show up, and what is more I hear they leave Manhattan, and are back in Brooklyn working every day handling beer. Naturally this is very surprising to me, because the way things are running beer is a tough dodge just now, and there is very little profit in same, and I figure that with the scratch they must make off Bookie Bob, Harry the Horse and Spanish John and Little Isadore have a right to be taking things easy.

Now one night I am in Good Time Charley Bernstein's little speak in Forty-eighth Street, talking of this and that with Charley, when in comes Harry the Horse, looking very weary and by no means prosperous. Naturally I give him a large hello, and by and by we get to gabbing together and I ask him whatever becomes of the Bookie Bob matter, and Harry the Horse tells me as follows:

Yes [Harry the Horse says], we snatch Bookie Bob all 9

right. In fact, we snatch him the very next night after we are talking to you, or on a Wednesday night. Our finger tells us Bookie Bob is going to a wake over in his old neighbourhood on Tenth Avenue, near Thirty-eighth Street, and this is where we pick him up.

He is leaving the place in his car along about midnight, and of course Bookie Bob is alone as he seldom lets anybody ride with him because of the wear and tear on his car cushions, and Little Isadore swings our flivver in front of him and makes him stop. Naturally Bookie Bob is greatly surprised when I poke my head into his car and tell him I wish the pleasure of his company for a short time, and at first he is inclined to argue the matter, saying I must make a mistake, but I put the old convincer on him by letting him peek down the snozzle of my John Roscoe.

We lock his car and throw the keys away, and then we take Bookie Bob in our car and go to a certain spot on Eighth Avenue where we have a nice little apartment all ready. When we get there I tell Bookie Bob that he can call up anybody he wishes and state that the snatch is on him and that it will require twenty-five G's, cash money, to take it off, but of course I also tell Bookie Bob that he is not to mention where he is or something may happen to him.

Well, I will say one thing for Bookie Bob, although everybody is always weighing in the sacks on him and saying he is no good – he takes it like a gentleman, and very calm and businesslike.

Furthermore, he does not seem alarmed, as many citizens

are when they find themselves in such a situation. He recognizes the justice of our claim at once, saying as follows:

'I will telephone my partner, Sam Salt,' he says. 'He is the only one I can think of who is apt to have such a sum as twenty-five G's cash money. But,' he says, 'if you gentlemen will pardon the question, because this is a new experience to me, how do I know everything will be okay for me after you get the scratch?'

'Why,' I say to Bookie Bob, somewhat indignant, 'it is well known to one and all in this town that my word is my bond. There are two things I am bound to do,' I say, 'and one is to keep my word in such a situation as this, and the other is to pay anything I owe a bookmaker, no matter what, for these are obligations of honour with me.'

'Well,' Bookie Bob says, 'of course I do not know you gentlemen, and, in fact, I do not remember ever seeing any of you, although your face is somewhat familiar, but if you pay your bookmaker you are an honest guy, and one in a million. In fact,' Bookie Bob says, 'if I have all the scratch that is owing to me around this town, I will not be telephoning anybody for such a sum as twenty-five G's. I will have such a sum in my pants pocket for change.'

Now Bookie Bob calls a certain number and talks to somebody there but he does not get Sam Salt, and he seems much disappointed when he hangs up the receiver again.

'This is a very tough break for me,' he says. 'Sam Salt goes to Atlantic City an hour ago on very important business and will not be back until to-morrow evening, and they do not know where he is to stay in Atlantic City. And,' Bookie Bob says, 'I cannot think of anybody else to call up to get this scratch, especially anybody I will care to have know I am in this situation.'

'Why not call your ever-loving wife?' I say. 'Maybe she can dig up this kind of scratch.'

'Say,' Bookie Bob says, 'you do not suppose I am chump enough to give my ever-loving wife twenty-five G's, or even let her know where she can get her dukes on twenty-five G's belonging to me, do you? I give my ever-loving wife ten bucks per week for spending money,' Bookie Bob says, 'and this is enough scratch for any doll, especially when you figure I pay for her meals.'

Well, there seems to be nothing we can do except wait until Sam Salt gets back, but we let Bookie Bob call his ever-loving wife, as Bookie Bob says he does not wish to have her worrying about his absence, and tells her a big lie about having to go to Jersey city to sit up with a sick Brother Elk.

Well, it is now nearly four o'clock in the morning, so we put Bookie Bob in a room with Little Isadore to sleep, although, personally, I consider making a guy sleep with Little Isadore very cruel treatment, and Spanish John and I take turns keeping awake and watching out that Bookie Bob does not take the air on us before paying us off. To tell the truth, Little Isadore and Spanish John are somewhat disappointed that Bookie Bob agreed to settle so promptly, because they are looking forward to tickling his feet with great relish.

Now Bookie Bob turns out to be very good company when he wakes up the next morning, because he knows a lot of race-track stories and plenty of scandal, and he keeps us much interested at breakfast. He talks along with us as if he knows us all his life, and he seems very nonchalant indeed, but the chances are he will not be so nonchalant if I tell him about Spanish John's thought.

Well, about noon Spanish John goes out of the apartment and comes back with a racing sheet, because he knows Little Isadore and I will be wishing to know what is running in different spots although we do not have anything to bet on these races, or any way of betting on them, because we are overboard with every bookmaker we know.

Now Bookie Bob is also much interested in the matter of what is running, especially at Belmont, and he is bending over the table with me and Spanish John and Little Isadore, looking at the sheet, when Spanish John speaks as follows:

'My goodness,' Spanish John says, 'a spot such as this fifth race with Questionnaire at four to five is like finding money in the street. I only wish I have a few bobs to bet on him at such a price,' Spanish John says.

'Why,' Bookie Bob says, very polite, 'if you gentlemen wish to bet on these races I will gladly book to you. It is a good way to pass away the time while we are waiting for Sam Salt, unless you will rather play pinochle?'

'But,' I say, 'we have no scratch to play the races, at least not much.'

'Well,' Bookie Bob says, 'I will take your markers, because I hear what you say about always paying your bookmaker, and you put yourself away with me as an honest guy, and these other gentlemen also impress me as honest guys.'

Now what happens but we begin betting Bookie Bob on 13

the different races, not only at Belmont, but at all the other tracks in the country, for Little Isadore and Spanish John and I are guys who like plenty of action when we start betting on the horses. We write out markers for whatever we wish to bet and hand them to Bookie Bob, and Bookie Bob sticks these markers in an inside pocket, and along in the late afternoon it looks as if he has a tumour on his chest.

We get the race results by 'phone off a poolroom downtown as fast as they come off, and also the prices, and it is a lot of fun, and Little Isadore and Spanish John and Bookie Bob and I are all little pals together until all the races are over and Bookie Bob takes out the markers and starts counting himself up.

It comes out then that I owe Bookie Bob ten G's, and Spanish John owes him six G's, and Little Isadore owes him four G's, as Little Isadore beats him a couple of races out west.

Well, about this time, Bookie Bob manages to get Sam Salt on the 'phone, and explains to Sam that he is to go to a certain safe-deposit box and get out twenty-five G's, and then wait until midnight and hire himself a taxicab and start riding around the block between Fifty-first and Fifty-second, from Eighth to Ninth Avenues, and to keep riding until somebody flags the cab and takes the scratch off him.

Naturally Sam Salt understands right away that the snatch is on Bookie Bob, and he agrees to do as he is told, but he says he cannot do it until the following night because he knows there is not twenty-five G's in the box, and he will have to get the difference at the track next day. So there we are with another day in the apartment and Spanish John and Little Isadore and I are just as well pleased because Bookie Bob has us hooked and we naturally wish to wiggle off.

But the next day is worse than ever. In all the years I am playing the horses I never have such a tough day, and Spanish John and Little Isadore are just as bad. In fact, we are all going so bad that Bookie Bob seems to feel sorry for us and often lays us a couple of points above the track prices, but it does no good. At the end of the day, I am in a total of twenty G's, while Spanish John owes fifteen, and Little Isadore fifteen, a total of fifty G's among the three of us. But we are never any hands to hold post-mortems on bad days, so Little Isadore goes out to a delicatessen store and lugs in a lot of nice things to eat, and we have a fine dinner, and then we sit around with Bookie Bob telling stories, and even singing a few songs together until time to meet Sam Salt.

When it comes on midnight Spanish John goes out and lays for Sam, and gets a little valise off of Sam Salt. Then Spanish John comes back to the apartment and we open the valise and the twenty-five G's are there okay, and we cut this scratch three ways.

Then I tell Bookie Bob he is free to go on about his business, and good luck to him, at that, but Bookie Bob looks at me as if he is very much surprised, and hurt, and says to me like this:

'Well, gentlemen, thank you for your courtesy, but what about the scratch you owe me? What about these markers? Surely, gentlemen, you will pay your bookmaker?'

Well, of course we owe Bookie Bob these markers, all right, and of course a man must pay his bookmaker, no matter what, so I hand over my bit and Bookie Bob puts down something in a little note-book that he takes out of his kick.

Then Spanish John and Little Isadore hand over their dough, too, and Bookie Bob puts down something more in the little note-book.

'Now,' Bookie Bob says, 'I credit each of your accounts with these payments, but you gentlemen still owe me a matter of twenty-five G's over and above the twenty-five I credit you with, and I hope and trust you will make arrangements to settle this at once because,' he says, 'I do not care to extend such accommodations over any considerable period.'

'But,' I say, 'we do not have any more scratch after paying you the twenty-five G's on account.'

'Listen,' Bookie Bob says, dropping his voice down to a whisper, 'what about putting the snatch on my partner, Sam Salt, and I will wait over a couple of days with you and keep booking to you, and maybe you can pull yourselves out. But of course,' Bookie Bob whispers, 'I will be entitled to twenty-five per cent. of the snatch for putting the finger on Sam for you.'

But Spanish John and Little Isadore are sick and tired of Bookie Bob and will not listen to staying in the apartment any longer, because they say he is a jinx to them and they cannot beat him in any manner, shape or form. Furthermore, I am personally anxious to get away because something Bookie Bob says reminds me of something.

It reminds me that besides the scratch we owe him, we forget to take out six G's two-fifty for the party who puts the finger on Bookie Bob for us, and this is a very serious matter indeed, because anybody will tell you that failing to pay a finger is considered a very dirty trick. Furthermore, if it gets around that you fail to pay a finger, nobody else will ever finger for you.

So [Harry the Horse says] we quit the snatching business because there is no use continuing while this obligation is outstanding against us, and we go back to Brooklyn to earn enough scratch to pay our just debts.

We are paying off Bookie Bob's IOU a little at a time, because we do not wish to ever have anybody say we welsh on a bookmaker, and furthermore we are paying off the six G's two-fifty commission we owe our finger.

And while it is tough going, I am glad to say our honest effort is doing somebody a little good, because I see Bookie Bob's ever-loving wife the other night all dressed up in new clothes and looking very happy, indeed.

And while a guy is telling me she is looking so happy because she gets a large legacy from an uncle who dies in Switzerland, and is now independent of Bookie Bob, I only hope and trust [Harry the Horse says] that it never gets out that our finger in this case is nobody but Bookie Bob's ever-loving wife.

Sense of Humour

One night I am standing in front of Mindy's restaurant on Broadway, thinking of practically nothing whatever, when all of a sudden I feel a very terrible pain in my left foot.

In fact, this pain is so very terrible that it causes me to leap up and down like a bullfrog, and to let out loud cries of agony, and to speak some very profane language, which is by no means my custom, although of course I recognize the pain as coming from a hot foot, because I often experience this pain before.

Furthermore, I know Joe the Joker must be in the neighbourhood, as Joe the Joker has the most wonderful sense of humour of anybody in this town, and is always around giving people the hot foot, and gives it to me more times than I can remember. In fact, I hear Joe the Joker invents the hot foot, and it finally becomes a very popular idea all over the country.

The way you give a hot foot is to sneak up behind some guy who is standing around thinking of not much, and stick a paper match in his shoe between the sole and the upper along about where his little toe ought to be, and then light the match. By and by the guy will feel a terrible pain in his foot, and will start stamping around, and hollering, and carrying on generally, and it is always a most comical sight and a wonderful laugh to one and all to see him suffer.

No one in the world can give a hot foot as good as Joe the Joker, because it takes a guy who can sneak up very quiet on the guy who is to get the hot foot, and Joe can sneak up so quiet many guys on Broadway are willing to lay you odds that he can give a mouse a hot foot if you can find a mouse that wears shoes. Furthermore, Joe the Joker can take plenty of care of himself in case the guy who gets the hot foot feels like taking the matter up, which sometimes happens, especially with guys who get their shoes made to order at forty bobs per copy and do not care to have holes burned in these shoes.

But Joe does not care what kind of shoes the guys are wearing when he feels like giving out hot foots, and furthermore, he does not care who the guys are, although many citizens think he makes a mistake the time he gives a hot foot to Frankie Ferocious. In fact, many citizens are greatly horrified by this action, and go around saying no good will come of it.

This Frankie Ferocious comes from over in Brooklyn, where he is considered a rising citizen in many respects, and by no means a guy to give hot foots to, especially as Frankie Ferocious has no sense of humour whatever. In fact, he is always very solemn, and nobody ever sees him laugh, and he certainly does not laugh when Joe the Joker gives him a hot foot one day on Broadway when Frankie Ferocious is standing talking over a business matter with some guys from the Bronx.

He only scowls at Joe, and says something in Italian, and while I do not understand Italian, it sounds so unpleasant 19 that I guarantee I will leave town inside of the next two hours if he says it to me.

Of course Frankie Ferocious's name is not really Ferocious, but something in Italian like Feroccio, and I hear he originally comes from Sicily, although he lives in Brooklyn for quite some years, and from a modest beginning he builds himself up until he is a very large operator in merchandise of one kind and another, especially alcohol. He is a big guy of maybe thirty-odd, and he has hair blacker than a yard up a chimney, and black eyes, and black eyebrows, and a slow way of looking at people.

Nobody knows a whole lot about Frankie Ferocious, because he never has much to say, and he takes his time saying it, but everybody gives him plenty of room when he comes around, as there are rumours that Frankie never likes to be crowded. As far as I am concerned, I do not care for any part of Frankie Ferocious, because his slow way of looking at people always makes me nervous, and I am always sorry Joe the Joker gives him a hot foot, because I figure Frankie Ferocious is bound to consider it a most disrespectful action, and hold it against everybody that lives on the Island of Manhattan.

But Joe the Joker only laughs when anybody tells him he is out of line in giving Frankie the hot foot, and says it is not his fault if Frankie has no sense of humour. Furthermore, Joe says he will not only give Frankie another hot foot if he gets a chance, but that he will give hot foots to the Prince of Wales or Mussolini, if he catches them in the right spot, although Regret, the horse player, states that Joe can have twenty to one any time that he will not give Mussolini any hot foots and get away with it.

Anyway, just as I suspect, there is Joe the Joker watching me when I feel the hot foot, and he is laughing very heartily, and furthermore, a large number of other citizens are also laughing heartily, because Joe the Joker never sees any fun in giving people the hot foot unless others are present to enjoy the joke.

Well, naturally when I see who it is gives me the hot foot I join in the laughter, and go over and shake hands with Joe, and when I shake hands with him there is more laughter, because it seems Joe has a hunk of Limburger cheese in his duke, and what I shake hands with is this Limburger. Furthermore, it is some of Mindy's Limburger cheese, and everybody knows Mindy's Limburger is very squashy, and also very loud.

Of course I laugh at this, too, although to tell the truth I will laugh much more heartily if Joe the Joker drops dead in front of me, because I do not like to be made the subject of laughter on Broadway. But my laugh is really quite hearty when Joe takes the rest of the cheese that is not on my fingers and smears it on the steering-wheels of some automobiles parked in front of Mindy's, because I get to thinking of what the drivers will say when they start steering their cars.

Then I get talking to Joe the Joker, and I ask him how things are up in Harlem, where Joe and his younger brother, Freddy, and several other guys have a small organization operating in beer, and Joe says things are as good as can be expected considering business conditions. Then I ask him how Rosa is getting along, this Rosa being Joe the Joker's ever-loving wife, and a personal friend of mine, as I know her when she is Rosa Midnight and is singing in the old Hot Box before Joe hauls off and marries her.

Well, at this question Joe the Joker starts laughing, and I can see that something appeals to his sense of humour, and finally he speaks as follows:

'Why,' he says, 'do you not hear the news about Rosa? She takes the wind on me a couple of months ago for my friend Frankie Ferocious, and is living in an apartment over in Brooklyn, right near his house, although,' Joe says, 'of course you understand I am telling you this only to answer your question, and not to holler copper on Rosa.'

Then he lets out another large ha-ha, and in fact Joe the Joker keeps laughing until I am afraid he will injure himself internally. Personally, I do not see anything comical in a guy's ever-loving wife taking the wind on him for a guy like Frankie Ferocious, so when Joe the Joker quiets down a bit I ask him what is funny about the proposition.

'Why,' Joe says, 'I have to laugh every time I think of how the big greaseball is going to feel when he finds out how expensive Rosa is. I do not know how many things Frankie Ferocious has running for him in Brooklyn,' Joe says, 'but he better try to move himself in on the mint if he wishes to keep Rosa going.'

Then he laughs again, and I consider it wonderful the way Joe is able to keep his sense of humour even in such a situation as this, although up to this time I always think Joe is very daffy indeed about Rosa, who is a little doll, weighing maybe ninety pounds with her hat on and quite cute.

Now I judge from what Joe the Joker tells me that Frankie Ferocious knows Rosa before Joe marries her and is always pitching to her when she is singing in the Hot Box, and even after she is Joe's ever-loving wife, Frankie occasionally calls her up, especially when he commences to be a rising citizen of Brooklyn, although of course Joe does not learn about these calls until later. And about the time Frankie Ferocious commences to be a rising citizen of Brooklyn, things begin breaking a little tough for Joe the Joker, what with the depression and all, and he has to economize on Rosa in spots, and if there is one thing Rosa cannot stand it is being economized on.

Along about now, Joe the Joker gives Frankie Ferocious the hot foot, and just as many citizens state at the time, it is a mistake, for Frankie starts calling Rosa up more than some-what, and speaking of what a nice place Brooklyn is to live in – which it is, at that – and between these boosts for Brooklyn and Joe the Joker's economy, Rosa hauls off and takes a subway to Borough Hall, leaving Joe a note telling him that if he does not like it he knows what he can do.

'Well, Joe,' I say, after listening to his story, 'I always hate to hear of these little domestic difficulties among my friends, but maybe this is all for the best. Still, I feel sorry for you, if it will do you any good,' I say.

'Do not feel sorry for me,' Joe says. 'If you wish to feel sorry for anybody, feel sorry for Frankie Ferocious, and,' he says, 'if you can spare a little more sorrow, give it to Rosa.'

And Joe the Joker laughs very hearty again and starts telling me about a little scatter that he has up in Harlem where he keeps a chair fixed up with electric wires so he can give anybody that sits down in it a nice jolt, which sounds very humorous to me, at that, especially when Joe tells me how they turn on too much juice one night and almost kill Commodore Jake.

Finally Joe says he has to get back to Harlem, but first he goes to the telephone in the corner cigar store and calls up Mindy's and imitates a doll's voice, and tells Mindy he is Peggy Joyce, or somebody, and orders fifty dozen sandwiches sent up at once to an apartment in West Seventy-second Street for a birthday party, although of course there is no such number as he gives, and nobody there will wish fifty dozen sandwiches if there is such a number.

Then Joe gets in his car and starts off, and while he is waiting for the traffic lights at Fiftieth Street, I see citizens on the sidewalks making sudden leaps, and looking around very fierce, and I know Joe the Joker is plugging them with pellets made out of tin foil, which he fires from a rubber band hooked between his thumb and forefinger.

Joe the Joker is very expert with this proposition, and it is very funny to see the citizens jump, although once or twice in his life Joe makes a miscue and knocks out somebody's eye. But it is all in fun, and shows you what a wonderful sense of humour Joe has.

Well, a few days later I see by the papers where a couple of Harlem guys Joe the Joker is mobbed up with are found

done up in sacks over in Brooklyn, very dead indeed, and the coppers say it is because they are trying to move in on certain business enterprises that belong to nobody but Frankie Ferocious. But of course the coppers do not say Frankie Ferocious puts these guys in the sacks, because in the first place Frankie will report them to Headquarters if the coppers say such a thing about him, and in the second place putting guys in sacks is strictly a St Louis idea and to have a guy put in a sack properly you have to send to St Louis for experts in this matter.

Now, putting a guy in a sack is not as easy as it sounds, and in fact it takes quite a lot of practice and experience. To put a guy in a sack properly, you first have to put him to sleep, because naturally no guy is going to walk into a sack wide awake unless he is a plumb sucker. Some people claim the best way to put a guy to sleep is to give him a sleeping powder of some kind in a drink, but the real experts just tap the guy on the noggin with a blackjack, which saves the expense of buying the drink.

Anyway, after the guy is asleep, you double him up like a pocketknife, and tie a cord or a wire around his neck and under his knees. Then you put him in a gunny sack, and leave him some place, and by and by when the guy wakes up and finds himself in the sack, naturally he wants to get out and the first thing he does is to try to straighten out his knees. This pulls the cord around his neck up so tight that after a while the guy is all out of breath.

So then when somebody comes along and opens the sack they find the guy dead, and nobody is responsible for this unfortunate situation, because after all the guy really commits 25 suicide, because if he does not try to straighten out his knees he may live to a ripe old age, if he recovers from the tap on the noggin.

Well, a couple of days later I see by the papers where three Brooklyn citizens are scragged as they are walking peaceably along Clinton Street, the scragging being done by some parties in an automobile who seem to have a machine gun, and the papers state that the citizens are friends of Frankie Ferocious, and that it is rumoured the parties with the machine gun are from Harlem.

I judge by this that there is some trouble in Brooklyn, especially as about a week after the citizens are scragged in Clinton Street, another Harlem guy is found done up in a sack like a Virginia ham near Prospect Park, and now who is it but Joe the Joker's brother, Freddy, and I know Joe is going to be greatly displeased by this.

By and by it gets so nobody in Brooklyn will open as much as a sack of potatoes without first calling in the gendarmes, for fear a pair of No. 8 shoes will jump out at them.

Now one night I see Joe the Joker, and this time he is all alone, and I wish to say I am willing to leave him all alone, because something tells me he is hotter than a stove. But he grabs me as I am going past, so naturally I stop to talk to him, and the first thing I say is how sorry I am about his brother.

'Well,' Joe the Joker says, 'Freddy is always a kind of a sap. Rosa calls him up and asks him to come over to Brooklyn to see her. She wishes to talk to Freddy about getting me to give her a divorce,' Joe says, 'so she can marry

Frankie Ferocious, I suppose. Anyway,' he says, 'Freddy tells Commodore Jake why he is going to see her. Freddy always likes Rosa, and thinks maybe he can patch it up between us. So,' Joe says, 'he winds up in a sack. They get him after he leaves her apartment. I do not claim Rosa will ask him to come over if she has any idea he will be sacked,' Joe says, 'but,' he says, 'she is responsible. She is a bad-luck doll.'

Then he starts to laugh, and at first I am greatly horrified, thinking it is because something about Freddy being sacked strikes his sense of humour, when he says to me, like this:

'Say,' he says, 'I am going to play a wonderful joke on Frankie Ferocious.'

'Well, Joe,' I say, 'you are not asking me for advice, but I am going to give you some free, gratis, and for nothing. Do not play any jokes on Frankie Ferocious, as I hear he has no more sense of humour than a nanny goat. I hear Frankie Ferocious will not laugh if you have Al Jolson, Eddie Cantor, Ed Wynn and Joe Cook telling him jokes all at once. In fact,' I say, 'I hear he is a tough audience.'

'Oh,' Joe the Joker says, 'he must have some sense of humour somewhere to stand for Rosa. I hear he is daffy about her. In fact, I understand she is the only person in the world he really likes, and trusts. But I must play a joke on him. I am going to have myself delivered to Frankie Ferocious in a sack.'

Well, of course I have to laugh at this myself, and Joe the Joker laughs with me. Personally, I am laughing just at the idea of anybody having themselves delivered to Frankie

Ferocious in a sack, and especially Joe the Joker, but of course I have no idea Joe really means what he says.

'Listen,' Joe says, finally. 'A guy from St Louis who is a friend of mine is doing most of the sacking for Frankie Ferocious. His name is Ropes McGonnigle. In fact,' Joe says, 'he is a very dear old pal of mine, and he has a wonderful sense of humour like me. Ropes McGonnigle has nothing whatever to do with sacking Freddy,' Joe says, 'and he is very indignant about it since he finds out Freddy is my brother, so he is anxious to help me play a joke on Frankie.

'Only last night,' Joe says, 'Frankie Ferocious sends for Ropes and tells him he will appreciate it as a special favour if Ropes will bring me to him in a sack. I suppose,' Joe says, 'that Frankie Ferocious hears from Rosa what Freddy is bound to tell her about my ideas on divorce. I have very strict ideas on divorce,' Joe says, 'especially where Rosa is concerned. I will see her in what's-this before I ever do her and Frankie Ferocious such a favour as giving her a divorce.

'Anyway,' Joe the Joker says, 'Ropes tells me about Frankie Ferocious propositioning him, so I send Ropes back to Frankie Ferocious to tell him he knows I am to be in Brooklyn to-morrow night, and furthermore, Ropes tells Frankie that he will have me in a sack in no time. And so he will,' Joe says.

'Well,' I say, 'personally, I see no percentage in being delivered to Frankie Ferocious in a sack, because as near as I can make out from what I read in the papers, there is no future for a guy in a sack that goes to Frankie Ferocious.

What I cannot figure out,' I say, 'is where the joke on Frankie comes in.'

'Why,' Joe the Joker says, 'the joke is, I will not be asleep in the sack, and my hands will not be tied, and in each of my hands I will have a John Roscoe, so when the sack is delivered to Frankie Ferocious and I pop out blasting away, can you not imagine his astonishment?'

Well, I can imagine this, all right. In fact when I get to thinking of the look of surprise that is bound to come to Frankie Ferocious's face when Joe the Joker comes out of the sack I have to laugh, and Joe the Joker laughs right along with me.

'Of course,' Joe says, 'Ropes McGonnigle will be there to start blasting with me, in case Frankie Ferocious happens to have any company.'

Then Joe the Joker goes on up the street, leaving me still laughing, from thinking of how amazed Frankie Ferocious will be when Joe bounces out of the sack and starts throwing slugs around and about. I do not hear of Joe from that time to this, but I hear the rest of the story from very reliable parties.

It seems that Ropes McGonnigle does not deliver the sack himself, after all, but sends it by an expressman to Frankie Ferocious's home. Frankie Ferocious receives many sacks such as this in his time, because it seems that it is a sort of passion with him to personally view the contents of the sacks and check up on them before they are distributed about the city, and of course Ropes McGonnigle knows about this passion from doing so much sacking for Frankie.

When the expressman takes the sack into Frankie's house, Frankie personally lugs it down into his basement, and there he outs with a big John Roscoe and fires six shots into the sack, because it seems Ropes McGonnigle tips him off to Joe the Joker's plan to pop out of the sack and start blasting.

I hear Frankie Ferocious has a very strange expression on his pan and is laughing the only laugh anybody ever hears from him when the gendarmes break in and put the arm on him for murder, because it seems that when Ropes McGonnigle tells Frankie of Joe the Joker's plan, Frankie tells Ropes what he is going to do with his own hands before opening the sack. Naturally, Ropes speaks to Joe the Joker of Frankie's idea about filling the sack full of slugs, and Joe's sense of humour comes right out again.

So, bound and gagged, but otherwise as right as rain in the sack that is delivered to Frankie Ferocious, is by no means Joe the Joker, but Rosa.

The Bloodhounds of Broadway

One morning along about four bells, I am standing in front
of Mindy's restaurant on Broadway with a guy by the name
of Regret, who has this name because it seems he wins a very
large bet the year the Whitney filly, Regret, grabs the Kentucky Derby, and can never forget it, which is maybe because
it is the only very large bet he ever wins in his life.

What this guy's real name is I never hear, and anyway
names make no difference to me, especially on Broadway,
because the chances are that no matter what name a guy has,
it is not his square name. So, as far as I am concerned,
Regret is as good a name as any other for this guy I am
talking about, who is a fat guy, and very gabby, though
generally he is talking about nothing but horses, and how he
gets beat three dirty noses the day before at Belmont, or
wherever the horses are running.

In all the years I know Regret he must get beat ten
thousand noses, and always they are dirty noses, to hear him
tell it. In fact, I never once hear him say he is beat a clean
nose, but of course this is only the way horse-racing guys
talk. What Regret does for a living besides betting on horses
I do not know, but he seems to do pretty well at it, because
he is always around and about, and generally well dressed,
and with a lot of big cigars sticking up out of his vest pocket.

It is generally pretty quiet on Broadway along about four

bells in the morning, because at such an hour the citizens are mostly in speakeasies, and night clubs, and on this morning I am talking about it is very quiet, indeed, except for a guy by the name of Marvin Clay hollering at a young doll because she will not get into a taxicab with him to go to his apartment. But of course Regret and I do not pay much attention to such a scene, except that Regret remarks that the young doll seems to have more sense than you will expect to see in a doll loose on Broadway at four bells in the morning, because it is well known to one and all that any doll who goes to Marvin Clay's apartment, either has no brains whatever, or wishes to go there.

This Marvin Clay is a very prominent society guy, who is a great hand for hanging out in night clubs, and he has plenty of scratch which comes down to him from his old man, who makes it out of railroads and one thing and another. But Marvin Clay is a most obnoxious character, being loud and ungentlemanly at all times, on account of having all this scratch, and being always very rough and abusive with young dolls such as work in night clubs, and who have to stand for such treatment from Marvin Clay because he is a very good customer.

He is generally in evening clothes, as he is seldom around and about except in the evening, and he is maybe fifty years old, and has a very ugly mugg, which is covered with blotches, and pimples, but of course a guy who has so much scratch as Marvin Clay does not have to be so very handsome, at that, and he is very welcome indeed wherever he goes on

Broadway. Personally, I wish no part of such a guy as

Marvin Clay, although I suppose in my time on Broadway I must see a thousand guys like him, and there will always be guys like Marvin Clay on Broadway as long as they have old men to make plenty of scratch out of railroads to keep them going.

Well, by and by Marvin Clay gets the doll in the taxicab, and away they go, and it is all quiet again on Broadway, and Regret and I stand there speaking of this and that, and one thing and another, when along comes a very strange-looking guy leading two very strange-looking dogs. The guy is so thin I figure he must be about two pounds lighter than a stack of wheats. He has a long nose, and a sad face, and he is wearing a floppy old black felt hat, and he has on a flannel shirt, and baggy corduroy pants, and a see-more coat, which is a coat that lets you see more hip pockets than coat.

Personally, I never see a stranger-looking guy on Broadway, and I wish to say I see some very strange-looking guys on Broadway in my day. But if the guy is strange-looking, the dogs are even stranger-looking because they have big heads, and jowls that hang down like an old-time faro bank dealer's, and long ears the size of bed sheets. Furthermore, they have wrinkled faces, and big, round eyes that seem so sad I half expect to see them bust out crying.

The dogs are a sort of black and yellow in colour, and have long tails, and they are so thin you can see their ribs sticking out of their hides. I can see at once that the dogs and the guy leading them can use a few hamburgers very nicely, but then so can a lot of other guys on Broadway at this time, leaving out the dogs.

Well, Regret is much interested in the dogs right away, because he is a guy who is very fond of animals of all kinds, and nothing will do but he must stop the guy and start asking questions about what sort of dogs they are, and in fact I am also anxious to hear myself, because while I see many a pooch in my time I never see anything like these.

'They is bloodhounds,' the sad-looking guy says in a very sad voice, and with one of these accents such as Southern guys always have. 'They is man-tracking bloodhounds from Georgia.'

Now of course both Regret and me know what bloodhounds are because we see such animals chasing Eliza across the ice in Uncle Tom's Cabin when we are young squirts, but this is the first time either of us meet up with any bloodhounds personally, especially on Broadway. So we get to talking quite a bit to the guy, and his story is as sad as his face, and makes us both feel very sorry for him.

In fact, the first thing we know we have him and the bloodhounds in Mindy's and are feeding one and all big steaks, although Mindy puts up an awful squawk about us bringing the dogs in, and asks us what we think he is running, anyway. When Regret starts to tell him, Mindy says never mind, but not to bring any more Shetland ponies into his joint again as long as we live.

Well, it seems that the sad-looking guy's name is John Wangle, and he comes from a town down in Georgia where his uncle is the high sheriff, and one of the bloodhounds' name is Nip, and the other Tuck, and they are both trained

34 from infancy to track down guys such as lags who escape

from the county pokey, and bad niggers, and one thing and another, and after John Wangle gets the kinks out of his belly on Mindy's steaks, and starts talking good, you must either figure him a high-class liar, or the hounds the greatest mantrackers the world ever sees.

Now, looking at the dogs after they swallow six big sirloins apiece, and a lot of matzoths, which Mindy has left over from the Jewish holidays, and a job lot of goulash from the dinner bill, and some other odds and ends, the best I can figure them is hearty eaters, because they are now lying down on the floor with their faces hidden behind their ears, and are snoring so loud you can scarcely hear yourself think.

How John Wangle comes to be in New York with these bloodhounds is quite a story, indeed. It seems that a New York guy drifts into John's old home town in Georgia when the bloodhounds are tracking down a bad nigger, and this guy figures it will be a wonderful idea to take John Wangle and the dogs to New York and hire them out to the movies to track down the villains in the pictures. But when they get to New York, it seems the movies have other arrangements for tracking down their villains, and the guy runs out of scratch and blows away, leaving John Wangle and the bloodhounds stranded.

So here John Wangle is with Nip and Tuck in New York, and they are all living together in one room in a tenement house over in West Forty-ninth Street, and things are pretty tough with them, because John does not know how to get back to Georgia unless he walks, and he hears the walking is no good south of Roanoke. When I ask him why he does not write to his uncle, the high sheriff down there in Georgia, John Wangle says, there are two reasons, one being that he cannot write, and the other that his uncle cannot read.

Then I ask him why he does not sell the bloodhounds, and he says it is because the market for bloodhounds is very quiet in New York, and furthermore if he goes back to Georgia without the bloodhounds his uncle is apt to knock his ears down. Anyway, John Wangle says he personally loves Nip and Tuck very dearly, and in fact he says it is only his great love for them that keeps him from eating one or the other and maybe both, the past week, when his hunger is very great indeed.

Well, I never before see Regret so much interested in any situation as he is in John Wangle and the bloodhounds, but personally I am getting very tired of them, because the one that is called Nip finally wakes up and starts chewing on my leg, thinking it is maybe more steak, and when I kick him in the snoot, John Wangle scowls at me, and Regret says only very mean guys are unkind to dumb animals.

But to show you that John Wangle and his bloodhounds are not so dumb, they come moseying along past Mindy's every morning after this at about the same time, and Regret is always there ready to feed them, although he now has to take the grub out on the sidewalk, as Mindy will not allow the hounds in the joint again. Naturally Nip and Tuck become very fond of Regret, but they are by no means as fond of him as John Wangle, because John is commencing to fat up very nicely, and the bloodhounds are also taking on

weight.

Now what happens but Regret does not show up in front of Mindy's for several mornings hand running, because it seems that Regret makes a very nice score for himself one day against the horses, and buys himself a brand-new tuxedo, and starts stepping out around the night clubs, and especially around Miss Missouri Martin's Three Hundred Club, where there are many beautiful young dolls who dance around with no more clothes on them than will make a pad for a crutch, and it is well known that Regret dearly loves such scenes.

Furthermore, I hear reports around and about of Regret becoming very fond of a doll by the name of Miss Lovey Lou, who works in Miss Missouri Martin's Three Hundred Club, and of him getting in some kind of a jam with Marvin Clay over this doll, and smacking Marvin Clay in the kisser, so I figure Regret is getting a little simple, as guys who hang around Broadway long enough are bound to do. Now, when John Wangle and Nip and Tuck come around looking for a hand-out, there is nothing much doing for them, as nobody else around Mindy's feels any great interest in bloodhounds, especially such interest as will cause them to buy steaks, and soon Nip and Tuck are commencing to look very sad again, and John Wangle is downcast more than somewhat.

It is early morning again, and warm, and a number of citizens are out in front of Mindy's as usual, breathing the fresh air, when along comes a police inspector by the name of McNamara, who is a friend of mine, with a bunch of plain-clothes coppers with him, and Inspector McNamara tells me he is on his way to investigate a situation in an apartment house over in West Fifty-fourth Street, about three blocks away, where it seems a guy is shot; and not having anything else to do, I go with them, although as a rule I do not care to associate with coppers, because it arouses criticism from other citizens.

Well, who is the guy who is shot but Marvin Clay, and he is stretched out on the floor of the living-room of his apartment in evening clothes, with his shirt front covered with blood, and after Inspector McNamara takes a close peek at him, he sees that Marvin Clay is plugged smack dab in the chest, and that he seems to be fairly dead. Furthermore, there seems to be no clue whatever to who does the shooting, and Inspector McNamara says it is undoubtedly a very great mystery, and will be duck soup for the newspapers, especially as they do not have a good shooting mystery for several days.

Well, of course all this is none of my business, but all of a sudden I happen to think of John Wangle and his bloodhounds, and it seems to me it will be a great opportunity for them, so I say to the Inspector as follows:

'Listen, Mac,' I say, 'there is a guy here with a pair of man-tracking bloodhounds from Georgia who are very expert in tracking down matters such as this, and,' I say, 'maybe they can track down the rascal who shoots Marvin Clay, because the trail must be hotter than mustard right now.'

Well, afterwards I hear there is much indignation over my suggestion, because many citizens feel that the party who shoots Marvin Clay is entitled to more consideration than being tracked with bloodhounds. In fact, some think the party is entitled to a medal, but this discussion does not come up until later.

Anyway, at first the Inspector does not think much of my idea, and the other coppers are very sceptical, and claim that the best way to do under the circumstances is to arrest everybody in sight and hold them as material witnesses for a month or so, but the trouble is there is nobody in sight to arrest at this time, except maybe me, and the Inspector is a broad-minded guy, and finally he says all right, bring on the bloodhounds.

So I hasten back to Mindy's, and sure enough John Wangle and Nip and Tuck are out on the sidewalk peering at every passing face in the hope that maybe one of these faces will belong to Regret. It is a very pathetic sight, indeed, but John Wangle cheers up when I explain about Marvin Clay to him, and hurries back to the apartment house with me so fast that he stretches Nip's neck a foot, and is pulling Tuck along on his stomach half the time.

Well, when we get back to the apartment, John Wangle leads Nip and Tuck up to Marvin Clay, and they snuffle him all over, because it seems bloodhounds are quite accustomed to dead guys. Then John Wangle unhooks their leashes, and yells something at them, and the hounds begin snuffling all around and about the joint, with Inspector McNamara and the other coppers watching with great interest. All of a sudden Nip and Tuck go busting out of the apartment and into the street, with John Wangle after them, and all the rest of us after John Wangle. They head across Fifty-fourth Street back to Broadway, and the next thing anybody knows they are doing plenty of snuffling around in front of Mindy's.

By and by they take off up Broadway with their snozzles to the sidewalk, and we follow them very excited, because even the coppers now admit that it seems to be a sure thing they are red hot on the trail of the party who shoots Marvin Clay. At first Nip and Tuck are walking, but pretty soon they break into a lope, and there we are loping after them, John Wangle, the Inspector, and me, and the coppers.

Naturally, such a sight as this attracts quite some attention as we go along from any citizens stirring at this hour, and by and by milkmen are climbing down off their wagons, and scavenger guys are leaving their trucks standing where they are, and newsboys are dropping everything, and one and all joining in the chase, so by the time we hit Broadway and Fifty-sixth there is quite a delegation following the hounds with John Wangle in front, just behind Nip and Tuck, and yelling at them now and then as follows:

'Hold to it, boys!'

At Fifty-sixth the hounds turn east off Broadway and stop at the door of what seems to be an old garage, this door being closed very tight, and Nip and Tuck seem to wish to get through this door, so the Inspector and the coppers kick the door open, and who is in the garage having a big crap game but many prominent citizens of Broadway. Naturally, these citizens are greatly astonished at seeing the bloodhounds, and the rest of us, especially the coppers, and they start running every which way trying to get out of the joint, because crap shooting is quite illegal in these parts.

But the Inspector only says Ah-ha, and starts jotting down names in a note-book as if it is something he will refer to later, and Nip and Tuck are out of the joint almost as soon as they get in and are snuffling on down Fifty-sixth. They stop at four more doors in Fifty-sixth Street along, and when the coppers kick open these doors they find they are nothing but speakeasies, although one is a hop joint, and the citizens in these places are greatly put out by the excitement, especially as Inspector McNamara keeps jotting down things in his note-book.

Finally the Inspector starts glaring very fiercely at the coppers with us, and anybody can see that he is much displeased to find so much illegality going on in this district, and the coppers are starting in to hate Nip and Tuck quite freely, and one copper says to me like this:

'Why,' he says, 'these mutts are nothing but stool pigeons.'

Well, naturally, the noise of John Wangle's yelling, and the gabble of the mob following the hounds makes quite a disturbance, and arouses many of the neighbours in the apartment houses and hotels in the side streets, especially as this is summer, and most everybody has their windows open.

In fact, we see many tousled heads poked out of windows, and hear guys and dolls inquiring as follows:

'What is going on?'

It seems that when word gets about that bloodhounds are tracking down a wrongdoer it causes great uneasiness all through the Fifties, and in fact I afterwards hear that three guys are taken to the Polyclinic suffering with broken ankles and several bruises from hopping out of windows in the hotels we pass in the chase, or from falling off of fire-escapes.

Well, all of a sudden Nip and Tuck swing back into   41

Seventh Avenue, and pop into the entrance of a small apartment house, and go tearing up the stairs to the first floor, and when we get there these bloodhounds are scratching vigorously at the door of Apartment B-2, and going woofle-woofle, and we are all greatly excited, indeed, but the door opens, and who is standing there but a doll by the name of Maud Milligan, who is well known to one and all as the ever-loving doll of Big Nig, the crap shooter, who is down in Hot Springs at this time taking the waters, or whatever it is guys take in Hot Springs.

Now, Maud Milligan is not such a doll as I will care to have any part of, being red-headed, and very stern, and I am glad Nip and Tuck do not waste any more time in her apartment than it takes for them to run through her living-room and across her bed, because Maud is commencing to put the old eye on such of us present as she happens to know. But Nip and Tuck are in and out of the joint before you can say scat, because it is only a two-room apartment, at that, and we are on our way down the stairs and back into Seventh Avenue again while Inspector McNamara is still jotting down something in his note-book.

Finally, where do these hounds wind up, with about four hundred citizens behind them, and everybody perspiring quite freely indeed from the exercise, but at the door of Miss Missouri Martin's Three Hundred Club, and the doorman, who is a guy by the name of Soldier Sweeney, tries to shoo them away, but Nip runs between the Soldier's legs and upsets him, and Tuck steps in the Soldier's eye in trotting over him, and most of the crowd behind the hounds tread on him in passing, so the old Soldier is pretty well flattened out at the finish.

Nip and Tuck are now more excited than somewhat, and are going zoople-zoople in loud voices as they bust into the Three Hundred Club with John Wangle and the law, and all these citizens behind them. There is a very large crowd present and Miss Missouri Martin is squatted on the back of a chair in the middle of the dance floor when we enter, and is about to start her show when she sees the mob surge in, and at first she is greatly pleased because she thinks new business arrives, and if there is anything Miss Missouri Martin dearly loves, it is new business.

But before she can say hello, sucker, or anything else whatever, Nip runs under her chair, thinking maybe he is a dachshund, and dumps Miss Missouri Martin on the dance floor, and she lays there squawking no little, while the next thing anybody knows, Nip and Tuck are over in one corner of the joint, and are eagerly crawling up and down a fat guy who is sitting there with a doll alongside of him, and who is the fat guy but Regret!

Well, as Nip and Tuck rush at Regret he naturally gets up to defend himself, but they both hit him at the same time, and over he goes on top of the doll who is with him, and who seems to be nobody but Miss Lovey Lou. She is getting quite a squashing with Regret's heft spread out over her, and she is screaming quite some, especially when Nip lets out a foot of tongue and washes her make-up off her face, reaching for Regret. In fact, Miss Lovey Lou seems to be more afraid of the bloodhounds than she does of being squashed to death, 43 for when John Wangle and I hasten to her rescue and pull her out from under Regret she is moaning as follows:

'Oh, do not let them devour me – I will confess.'

Well, as nobody but me and John Wangle seem to hear this crack, because everybody else is busy trying to split out Regret and the bloodhounds, and as John Wangle does not seem to understand what Miss Lovey Lou is mumbling about, I shove her off into the crowd, and on back into the kitchen, which is now quite deserted, what with all the help being out watching the muss in the corner, and I say to her like this:

'What is it you confess?' I say. 'Is it about Marvin Clay?'

'Yes,' she says. 'It is about him. He is a pig,' she says. 'I shoot him, and I am glad of it. He is not satisfied with what he does to me two years ago, but he tries his deviltry on my baby sister. He has her in his apartment and when I find it out and go to get her, he says he will not let her go. So I shoot him. With my brother's pistol,' she says, 'and I take my baby sister home with me, and I hope he is dead, and gone where he belongs.'

'Well, now,' I say, 'I am not going to give you any argument as to where Marvin Clay belongs, but,' I say, 'you skip out of here and go on home, and wait until we can do something about this situation, while I go back and help Regret, who seems to be in a tough spot.'

'Oh, do not let these terrible dogs eat him up,' she says, and with this she takes the breeze and I return to the other room to find there is much confusion indeed, because it seems that Regret is now very indignant at Nip and Tuck, especially when he discovers that one of them plants his big old paw right on the front of Regret's shirt bosom, leaving a dirty mark. So when he struggles to his feet, Regret starts letting go with both hands, and he is by no means a bad puncher for a guy who does not do much punching as a rule. In fact, he flattens Nip with a right-hand to the jaw, and knocks Tuck plumb across the room with a left hook.

Well, poor Tuck slides over the slick dance floor into Miss Missouri Martin just as she is getting to her feet again, and bowls her over once more, but Miss Missouri Martin is also indignant by this time, and she gets up and kicks Tuck in a most unladylike manner. Of course, Tuck does not know so much about Miss Martin, but he is pretty sure his old friend Regret is only playing with him, so back he goes to Regret with his tongue out, and his tail wagging, and there is no telling how long this may go on if John Wangle does not step in and grab both hounds, while Inspector McNamara puts the arm on Regret and tells him he is under arrest for shooting Marvin Clay.

Well, of course everybody can see at once that Regret must be the guilty party all right, especially when it is remembered that he once had trouble with Marvin Clay, and one and all present are looking at Regret in great disgust, and saying you can see by his face that he is nothing but a degenerate type.

Furthermore, Inspector McNamara makes a speech to Miss Missouri Martin's customers in which he congratulates John Wangle and Nip and Tuck on their wonderful work in tracking down this terrible criminal and at the same time putting in a few boosts for the police department, while 45

Regret stands there paying very little attention to what the Inspector is saying, but trying to edge himself over close enough to Nip and Tuck to give them the old foot.

Well, the customers applaud what Inspector McNamara says, and Miss Missouri Martin gets up a collection of over two C's for John Wangle and his hounds, not counting what she holds out for herself. Also the chef comes forward and takes John Wangle and Nip and Tuck back into the kitchen and stuffs them full of food, although personally I will just as soon not have any of the food they serve in the Three Hundred Club.

They take Regret to the jail-house, and he does not seem to understand why he is under arrest, but he knows it has something to do with Nip and Tuck and he tries to bribe one of the coppers to put the bloodhounds in the same cell with him for awhile, though naturally the copper will not consider such a proposition. While Regret is being booked at the jail-house, word comes around that Marvin Clay is not only not dead, but the chances are he will get well, which he finally does, at that.

Moreover, he finally bails Regret out, and not only refuses to prosecute him but skips the country as soon as he is able to move, although Regret lays in the sneezer for several weeks, at that, never letting on after he learns the real situation that he is not the party who plugs Marvin Clay. Naturally, Miss Lovey Lou is very grateful to Regret for his wonderful sacrifice, and will no doubt become his ever-loving wife in a minute, if Regret thinks to ask her, but it seems Regret finds himself brooding so much over the idea of an ever-loving wife who is so handy with a Roscoe that he never really asks.

In the meantime, John Wangle and Nip and Tuck go back to Georgia on the dough collected by Miss Missouri Martin, and with a big reputation as man-trackers. So this is all there is to the story, except that one night I run into Regret with a suitcase in his hand, and he is perspiring very freely, although it is not so hot, at that, and when I ask him if he is going away, he says this is indeed his general idea. Moreover, he says he is going very far away. Naturally, I ask him why this is, and Regret says to me as follows:

'Well,' he says, 'ever since Big Nig, the crap shooter, comes back from Hot Springs, and hears how the blood-hounds track the shooter of Marvin Clay, he is walking up and down looking at me out of the corner of his eye. In fact,' Regret says, 'I can see that Big Nig is studying something over in his mind, and while Big Nig is a guy who is not such a fast thinker as others, I am afraid he may finally think himself to a bad conclusion.

'I am afraid,' Regret says, 'that Big Nig will think himself to the conclusion that Nip and Tuck are tracking me instead of the shooter, as many evil-minded guys are already whispering around and about, and that he may get the wrong idea about the trail leading to Maud Milligan's door.'

It Comes Up Mud

Personally, I never criticize Miss Beulah Beauregard for breaking her engagement to Little Alfie, because from what she tells me becomes engaged to him under false pretences, and I do not approve of guys using false pretences on dolls, except, of course, when nothing else will do.

It seems that Little Alfie promises to show Miss Beulah Beauregard the life of Riley following the races with him when he gets her to give up a first-class job displaying her shape to the customers in the 900 Club, although Miss Beulah Beauregard frankly admits that Little Alfie does not say what Riley, and afterward Little Alfie states that he must be thinking of Four-eyes Riley when he makes the promise, and everybody knows that Four-eyes Riley is nothing but a bum, in spades.

Anyway, the life Little Alfie shows Miss Beulah Beauregard after they become engaged is by no means exciting, according to what she tells me, as Little Alfie is always going around the race tracks with one or two crocodiles that he calls race horses, trying to win a few bobs for himself, and generally Little Alfie is broke and struggling, and Miss Beulah Beauregard says this is no existence for a member of a proud old Southern family such as the Beauregards.

In fact, Miss Beulah Beauregard often tells me that she has half a mind to leave Little Alfie and return to her ancestral home in Georgia, only she can never think of any way of getting there without walking, and Miss Beulah Beauregard says it always makes her feet sore to walk very far, although the only time anybody ever hears of Miss Beulah Beauregard doing much walking is the time she is shell-roaded on the Pelham Parkway by some Yale guys when she gets cross with them.

It seems that when Little Alfie is first canvassing Miss Beulah Beauregard to be his fiancée he builds her up to expect diamonds and furs and limousines and one thing and another, but the only diamond she ever sees is an engagement hoop that Little Alfie gives her as the old convincer when he happens to be in the money for a moment, and it is a very small diamond, at that, and needs a high north light when you look at it.

But Miss Beulah Beauregard treasures this diamond very highly just the same, and one reason she finally breaks off her engagement to Little Alfie is because he borrows the diamond one day during the Hialeah meeting at Miami without mentioning the matter to her, and hocks it for five bobs which he bets on an old caterpillar of his by the name of Governor Hicks to show.

Well, the chances are Miss Beulah Beauregard will not mind Little Alfie's borrowing the diamond so much if he does not take the twenty-five bobs he wins when Governor Hicks drops in there in the third hole and sends it to Colonel Matt Winn in Louisville to enter a three-year-old of his by the name of Last Hope in the Kentucky Derby, this Last Hope being the only other horse Little Alfie owns at this time. 49

Such an action makes Miss Beulah Beauregard very indignant indeed, because she says a babe in arms will know Last Hope cannot walk a mile and a quarter, which is the Derby distance, let alone run so far, and that even if Last Hope can run a mile and a quarter, he cannot run it fast enough to get up a sweat.

In fact, Miss Beulah Beauregard and Little Alfie have words over this proposition, because Little Alfie is very high on Last Hope and will not stand for anybody insulting this particular horse, not even his fiancée, although he never seems to mind what anybody says about Governor Hicks, and, in fact, he often says it himself.

Personally, I do not understand what Little Alfie sees in Last Hope, because the horse never starts more than once or twice since it is born, and then has a tough time finishing last, but Little Alfie says the fifty G's that Colonel Winn gives to the winner of the Kentucky Derby is just the same as in the jug in his name, especially if it comes up mud on Derby Day, for Little Alfie claims that Last Hope is bred to just naturally eat mud.

Well, Miss Beulah Beauregard says there is no doubt Little Alfie blows his topper, and that there is no percentage in her remaining engaged to a crack-pot, and many citizens put in with her on her statement because they consider entering Last Hope in the Derby very great foolishness, no matter if it comes up mud or what, and right away Tom Shaw offers 1,000 to 1 against the horse in the future book, and everybody says Tom is underlaying the price at that.

Miss Beulah Beauregard states that she is very discouraged

by the way things turn out, and that she scarcely knows what to do, because she fears her shape changes so much in the four or five years she is engaged to Little Alfie that the customers at the 900 Club may not care to look at it any more, especially if they have to pay for this privilege, although personally I will pay any reasonable cover charge to look at Miss Beulah Beauregard's shape any time, if it is all I suspect. As far as I can see it is still a very nice shape indeed, if you care for shapes.

Miss Beulah Beauregard is at this time maybe twenty-five or twenty-six, and is built like a first baseman, being tall and rangy. She has hay-coloured hair, and blue eyes, and lots of health, and a very good appetite. In fact, I once see Miss Beulah Beauregard putting on the fried chicken in the Seven Seas Restaurant in a way that greatly astonishes me, because I never knew before that members of proud old Southern families are such hearty eaters. Furthermore, Miss Beulah Beauregard has a very Southern accent, which makes her sound quite cute, except maybe when she is a little excited and is putting the zing on somebody, such as Little Alfie.

Well, Little Alfie says he regrets exceedingly that Miss Beulah Beauregard sees fit to break their engagement, and will not be with him when he cuts up the Derby dough, as he is planning a swell wedding for her at French Lick after the race, and even has a list all made out of the presents he is going to buy her, including another diamond, and now he has all this bother of writing out the list for nothing.

Furthermore, Little Alfie says he is so accustomed to having Miss Beulah Beauregard as his fiancée that he scarcely knows what to do without her, and he goes around with a very sad puss, and is generally quite low in his mind, because there is no doubt that Little Alfie loves Miss Beulah Beauregard more than somewhat.

But other citizens are around stating that the real reason Miss Beulah Beauregard breaks her engagement to Little Alfie is because a guy by the name of Mr Paul D. Veere is making a powerful play for her, and she does not wish him to know that she has any truck with a character such as Little Alfie, for of course Little Alfie is by no means anything much to look at, and, furthermore, what with hanging out with his horses most of the time, he never smells like any rose geranium.

It seems that this Mr Paul D. Veere is a New York banker, and he has a little moustache, and plenty of coconuts, and Miss Beulah Beauregard meets up with him one morning when she is displaying her shape on the beach at the Roney Plaza for nothing, and it also seems that there is enough of her shape left to interest Mr Paul D. Veere no little.

In fact, the next thing anybody knows, Mr Paul D. Veere is taking Miss Beulah Beauregard here and there, and around and about, although at this time Miss Beulah Beauregard is still engaged to Little Alfie, and the only reason Little Alfie does not notice Mr Paul D. Veere at first is because he is busy training Last Hope to win the Kentucky Derby, and hustling around trying to get a few bobs together every day to stand off the overhead, including Miss Beulah Beauregard, because naturally Miss Beulah Beauregard cannot bear the idea of living in a fleabag, such as the place where Little Alfie resides, but has to have a nice room at the Roney Plaza.

Well, personally, I have nothing against bankers as a class, and in fact I never meet up with many bankers in my life, but somehow I do not care for Mr Paul D. Veere's looks. He looks to me like a stony-hearted guy, although, of course, nobody ever sees any banker who does not look stony-hearted, because it seems that being bankers just naturally makes them look this way.

But Mr Paul D. Veere is by no means an old guy, and the chances are he speaks of something else besides horses to Miss Beulah Beauregard, and furthermore he probably does not smell like horses all the time, so nobody can blame Miss Beulah Beauregard for going around and about with him, although many citizens claim she is a little out of line in accepting Mr Paul D. Veere's play while she is still engaged to Little Alfie. In fact, there is great indignation in some circles about this, as many citizens feel that Miss Beulah Beauregard is setting a bad example to other fiancées.

But after Miss Beulah Beauregard formally announces that their engagement is off, it is agreed by one and all that she has a right to do as she pleases, and that Little Alfie himself gets out of line in what happens at Hialeah a few days later when he finally notices that Miss Beulah Beauregard seems to be with Mr Paul D. Veere, and on very friendly terms with him, at that. In fact, Little Alfie comes upon Mr Paul D. Veere in the act of kissing Miss Beulah Beauregard behind a hibiscus bush out near the paddock, and this scene is most revolting to Little Alfie as he never cares for hibiscus, anyway.

He forgets that Miss Beulah Beauregard is no longer his fiancée, and tries to take a punch at Mr Paul D. Veere, but he is stopped by a number of detectives, who are greatly horrified at the idea of anybody taking a punch at a guy who has as many coco-nuts as Mr Paul D. Veere, and while they are expostulating with Little Alfie, Miss Beulah Beauregard disappears from the scene and is observed no more in Miami. Furthermore, Mr Paul D. Veere also disappears, but of course nobody minds this very much, and, in fact, his disappearance is a great relief to all citizens who have fiancées in Miami at this time.

But it seems that before he disappears Mr Paul D. Veere calls on certain officials of the Jockey Club and weighs in the sacks on Little Alfie, stating that he is a most dangerous character to have loose around a race track, and naturally the officials are bound to listen to a guy who has as many coco-nuts as Mr Paul D. Veere.

So a day or two later old Cap Duhaine, the head detective around the race track, sends for Little Alfie and asks him what he thinks will become of all the prominent citizens such as bankers if guys go around taking punches at them and scaring them half to death, and Little Alfie cannot think of any answer to this conundrum off-hand, especially as Cap Duhaine then asks Little Alfie if it will be convenient for him to take his two horses elsewhere.

Well, Little Alfie can see that Cap Duhaine is hinting in a
polite way that he is not wanted around Hialeah any more,

and Little Alfie is a guy who can take a hint as well as the next guy, especially when Cap Duhaine tells him in confidence that the racing stewards do not seem able to get over the idea that some scalawag slips a firecracker into Governor Hicks the day old Governor Hicks runs third, because it seems from what Cap Duhaine says that the stewards consider it practically supernatural for Governor Hicks to run third anywhere, any time.

So there Little Alfie is in Miami, as clean as a jaybird, with two horses on his hands, and no way to ship them to any place where horses are of any account, and it is quite a predicament indeed, and causes Little Alfie to ponder quite some. And the upshot of his pondering is that Little Alfie scrapes up a few bobs here and there, and a few oats, and climbs on Governor Hicks one day and boots him in the slats and tells him to giddyup, and away he goes out of Miami, headed north, riding Governor Hicks and leading Last Hope behind him on a rope.

Naturally, this is considered a most unusual spectacle by one and all who witness it and, in fact, it is the first time anybody can remember a horse owner such as Little Alfie riding one of his own horses off in this way, and Gloomy Gus is offering to lay plenty of 5 to 1 that Governor Hicks never makes Palm Beach with Little Alfie up, as it is well known that the old Governor has bum legs and is half out of wind and is apt to pig it any time.

But it seems that Governor Hicks makes Palm Beach all right with Little Alfie up and going so easy that many citizens are around asking Gloomy for a price against Jacksonville. 55

Furthermore, many citizens are now saying that Little Alfie is a pretty smart guy, at that, to think of such an economical idea, and numerous other horse owners are looking their stock over to see if they have anything to ride up north themselves.

Many citizens are also saying that Little Alfie gets a great break when Miss Beulah Beauregard runs out on him, because it takes plenty of weight off him in the way of railroad fare and one thing and another; but it seems Little Alfie does not feel this way about the matter at all.

It seems that Little Alfie often thinks about Miss Beulah Beauregard as he goes jogging along to the north, and sometimes he talks to Governor Hicks and Last Hope about her, and especially to Last Hope, as Little Alfie always considers Governor Hicks somewhat dumb. Also Little Alfie sometimes sings sad love songs right out loud as he is riding along, although the first time he starts to sing he frightens Last Hope and causes him to break loose from the lead rope and run away, and Little Alfie is an hour catching him. But after this Last Hope gets so he does not mind Little Alfie's voice so much, except when Little Alfie tries to hit high C.

Well, Little Alfie has a very nice ride, at that, because the weather is fine and the farmers along the road feed him and his horses, and he has nothing whatever to worry about except a few saddle galls, and about getting to Kentucky for the Derby in May, and here it is only late in February, and anyway Little Alfie does not figure to ride any farther than maybe Maryland where he is bound to make a scratch so he can ship from there.

Now, one day Little Alfie is riding along a road through a stretch of piny woods, a matter of maybe ninety-odd miles north of Jacksonville, which puts him in the State of Georgia, when he passes a half-ploughed field on one side of the road near a ramshackly old house and beholds a most unusual scene:

A large white mule hitched to a plough is sitting down in the field and a tall doll in a sunbonnet and a gingham dress is standing beside the mule crying very heartily.

Naturally, the spectacle of a doll in distress, or even a doll who is not in distress, is bound to attract Little Alfie's attention, so he tells Governor Hicks and Last Hope to whoa, and then he asks the doll what is eating her, and the doll looks up at him out of her sunbonnet, and who is this doll but Miss Beulah Beauregard.

Of course Little Alfie is somewhat surprised to see Miss Beulah Beauregard crying over a mule, and especially in a sunbonnet, so he climbs down off of Governor Hicks to inquire into this situation, and right away Miss Beulah Beauregard rushes up to Little Alfie and chucks herself into his arms and speaks as follows:

'Oh, Alfie,' Miss Beulah Beauregard says, 'I am so glad you find me. I am thinking of you day and night, and wondering if you forgive me. Oh, Alfie, I love you,' she says. 'I am very sorry I go away with Mr Paul D. Veere. He is nothing but a great rapscallion,' she says. 'He promises to make me his ever-loving wife when he gets me to accompany him from Miami to his shooting-lodge on the Altamaha River, twenty-five miles from here, although,' she says, 'I never know before he has such a lodge in these parts.

'And,' Miss Beulah Beauregard says, 'the very first day I have to pop him with a pot of cold cream and render him half unconscious to escape his advances. Oh, Alfie,' she says, 'Mr Paul D. Veere's intentions towards me are by no means honourable. Furthermore,' she says, 'I learn he already has an ever-loving wife and three children in New York.'

Well, of course Little Alfie is slightly perplexed by this matter and can scarcely think of anything much to say, but finally he says to Miss Beulah Beauregard like this:

'Well,' he says, 'but what about the mule?'

'Oh,' Miss Beulah Beauregard says, 'his name is Abimelech, and I am ploughing with him when he hauls off and sits down and refuses to budge. He is the only mule we own,' she says, 'and he is old and ornery, and nobody can do anything whatever with him when he wishes to sit down. But,' she says, 'my papa will be very angry because he expects me to get this field all ploughed up by supper-time. In fact,' Miss Beulah Beauregard says, 'I am afraid my papa will be so angry he will give me a whopping, because he by no means forgives me as yet for coming home, and this is why I am shedding tears when you come along.'

Then Miss Beulah Beauregard begins crying again as if her heart will break, and if there is one thing Little Alfie hates and despises it is to see a doll crying, and especially Miss Beulah Beauregard, for Miss Beulah Beauregard can cry in a way to wake the dead when she is going good, so Little Alfie holds her so close to his chest he ruins four cigars in his vest pocket, and speaks to her as follows:

'Tut, tut,' Little Alfie says. 'Tut, tut, tut, tut, tut,' he says.

'Dry your eyes and we will just hitch old Governor Hicks here to the plough and get this field ploughed quicker than you can say scat, because,' Little Alfie says, 'when I am a young squirt, I am the best plougher in Columbia County, New York.'

Well, this idea cheers Miss Beulah Beauregard up no little, and so Little Alfie ties Last Hope to a tree and takes the harness off Abimelech, the mule, who keeps right on sitting down as if he does not care what happens, and puts the harness on Governor Hicks and hitches Governor Hicks to the plough, and the way the old Governor carries on when he finds out they wish him to pull a plough is really most surprising. In fact, Little Alfie has to get a club and reason with Governor Hicks before he will settle down and start pulling the plough.

It turns out that Little Alfie is a first-class plougher, at that, and while he is ploughing, Miss Beulah Beauregard walks along with him and talks a blue streak, and Little Alfie learns more things from her in half an hour than he ever before suspects in some years, and especially about Miss Beulah Beauregard herself.

It seems that the ramshackly old house is Miss Beulah Beauregard's ancestral home, and that her people are very poor, and live in these piny woods for generations, and that their name is Benson and not Beauregard at all, this being nothing but a name that Miss Beulah Beauregard herself thinks up out of her own head when she goes to New York to display her shape.

Furthermore, when they go to the house it comes out that 59

Miss Beulah Beauregard's papa is a tall, skinny old guy with a goatee, who can lie faster than Little Alfie claims Last Hope can run. But it seems that the old skeezicks takes quite an interest in Last Hope when Little Alfie begins telling him what a great horse this horse is, especially in the mud, and how he is going to win the Kentucky Derby.

In fact, Miss Beulah Beauregard's papa seems to believe everything Little Alfie tells him, and as he is the first guy Little Alfie ever meets up with who believes anything he tells about anything whatever, it is a privilege and a pleasure for Little Alfie to talk to him. Miss Beulah Beauregard also has a mamma who turns out to be very fat, and full of Southern hospitality, and quite handy with a skillet.

Then there is a grown brother by the name of Jeff, who is practically a genius, as he knows how to disguise skimmin's so it makes a person only a little sick when they drink it, this skimmin's being a drink which is made from skimmings that come to the top on boiling sugar cane, and generally it tastes like gasoline, and is very fatal indeed.

Now, the consequences are Little Alfie finds this place very pleasant, and he decides to spend a few weeks there, paying for his keep with the services of Governor Hicks as a plough horse, especially as he is now practically engaged to Miss Beulah Beauregard all over again and she will not listen to him leaving without her. But they have no money for her railroad fare, and Little Alfie becomes very indignant when she suggests she can ride Last Hope on north while he is riding Governor Hicks, and wishes to know if she thinks a Derby candidate can be used for a truck horse.

Well, this almost causes Miss Beulah Beauregard to start breaking the engagement all over again, as she figures it is a dirty crack about her heft, but her papa steps in and says they must remain until Governor Hicks get through with the ploughing anyway, or he will know the reason why. So Little Alfie stays and he puts in all his spare time training Last Hope and wondering who he can write to for enough dough to send Miss Beulah Beauregard north when the time comes.

He trains Last Hope by walking him and galloping him along the country roads in person, and taking care of him as if he is a baby, and what with this work, and the jog up from Miami, Last Hope fills out very strong and hearty, and anybody must admit that he is not a bad-looking beetle, though maybe a little more leggy than some like to see.

Now, it comes a Sunday, and all day long there is a very large storm with rain and wind that takes to knocking over big trees, and one thing and another, and no one is able to go outdoors much. So late in the evening Little Alfie and Miss Beulah Beauregard and all the Bensons are gathered about the stove in the kitchen drinking skimmin's, and Little Alfie is telling them all over again about how Last Hope will win the Kentucky Derby, especially if it comes up mud, when they hear a hammering at the door.

When the door is opened, who comes in but Mr Paul D. Veere, sopping wet from head to foot, including his little moustache, and limping so he can scarcely walk, and naturally his appearance nonplusses Miss Beulah Beauregard and Little Alfie, who can never forget that Mr Paul D. Veere is largely responsible for the saddle galls he gets riding up from Miami.

In fact, several times since he stops at Miss Beulah Beauregard's ancestral home, Little Alfie thinks of Mr Paul D. Veere, and every time he thinks of him he is in favour of going over to Mr Paul D. Veere's shooting-lodge on the Altamaha and speaking to him severely.

But Miss Beulah Beauregard always stops him, stating that the proud old Southern families in this vicinity are somewhat partial to the bankers and other rich guys from the North who have shooting-lodges around and about in the piny woods, and especially on the Altamaha, because these guys furnish a market to the local citizens for hunting guides, and corn liquor, and one thing and another.

Miss Beulah Beauregard says if a guest of the Bensons speaks to Mr Paul D. Veere severely, it may be held against the family, and it seems that the Benson family cannot stand any more beefs against it just at this particular time. So Little Alfie never goes, and here all of a sudden is Mr Paul D. Veere right in his lap.

Naturally, Little Alfie steps forward and starts winding up a large right hand with the idea of parking it on Mr Paul D. Veere's chin, but Mr Paul D. Veere seems to see that there is hostility afoot, and he backs up against the wall, and raises his hand, and speaks as follows.

'Folks,' Mr Paul D. Veere says, 'I just go into a ditch in my automobile half a mile up the road. My car is a wreck,' he says, 'and my right leg seems so badly hurt I am just barely
able to drag myself here. Now, folks,' he says, 'it is almost a

matter of life and death with me to get to the station at Tillinghast in time to flag the Orange Blossom Special. It is the last train tonight to Jacksonville, and I must be in Jacksonville before midnight so I can hire an aeroplane and get to New York by the time my bank opens at ten o'clock in the morning. It is about ten hours by plane from Jacksonville to New York,' Mr Paul D. Veere says, 'so if I can catch the Orange Blossom, I will be able to just about make it!'

Then he goes on speaking in a low voice and states that he receives a telephone message from New York an hour or so before at his lodge telling him he must hurry home, and right away afterward, while he is trying to telephone the station at Tillinghast to make sure they will hold the Orange Blossom until he gets there, no matter what, all the telephone and telegraph wires around and about go down in the storm.

So he starts for the station in his car, and just as it looks as if he may make it, his car runs smack-dab into a ditch and Mr Paul D. Veere's leg is hurt so there is no chance he can walk the rest of the way to the station, and there Mr Paul D. Veere is.

'It is a very desperate case, folks,' Mr Paul D. Veere says. 'Let me take your automobile, and I will reward you liberally.'

Well, at this Miss Beulah Beauregard's papa looks at a clock on the kitchen wall and states as follows:

'We do not keep an automobile, neighbour,' he says, 'and anyway,' he says, 'it is quite a piece from here to Tillinghast and the Orange Blossom is due in ten minutes, so I do not see how you can possibly make it. Rest your hat, neighbour,'

Miss Beulah Beauregard's papa says, 'and have some skim-min's, and take things easy, and I will look at your leg and see how bad you are bunged up.'

Well, Mr Paul D. Veere seems to turn as pale as a pillow as he hears this about the time, and then he says:

'Lend me a horse and buggy,' he says. 'I must be in New York in person in the morning. No one else will do but me,' he says, and as he speaks these words he looks at Miss Beulah Beauregard and then at Little Alfie as if he is speaking to them personally, although up to this time he does not look at either of them after he comes into the kitchen.

'Why, neighbour,' Miss Beulah Beauregard's papa says, 'we do not keep a buggy, and even if we do keep a buggy we do not have time to hitch up anything to a buggy. Neighbour,' he says, 'you are certainly on a bust if you think you can catch the Orange Blossom now.'

'Well, then,' Mr Paul D. Veere says, very sorrowful, 'I will have to go to jail.'

Then he flops himself down in a chair and covers his face with his hands, and he is a spectacle such as is bound to touch almost any heart, and when she sees him in this state Miss Beulah Beauregard begins crying because she hates to see anybody as sorrowed up as Mr Paul D. Veere, and between sobs she asks Little Alfie to think of something to do about the situation.

'Let Mr Paul D. Veere ride Governor Hicks to the station,' Miss Beauregard says. 'After all,' she says, 'I cannot forget his courtesy in sending me half-way here in his car from his shooting-lodge after I pop him with the pot of cold cream, instead of making me walk as those Yale guys do the time they red-light me.'

'Why,' Little Alfie says, 'it is a mile and a quarter from the gate out here to the station. I know,' he says, 'because I get a guy in an automobile to clock it on his meter one day last week, figuring to give Last Hope a workout over the full Derby route pretty soon. The road must be fetlock deep in mud at this time, and,' Little Alfie says, 'Governor Hicks cannot as much as stand up in the mud. The only horse in the world that can run fast enough through this mud to make the Orange Blossom is Last Hope, but,' Little Alfie says, 'of course I'm not letting anybody ride a horse as valuable as Last Hope to catch trains.'

Well, at this Mr Paul D. Veere lifts his head and looks at Little Alfie with great interest and speaks as follows:

'How much is this valuable horse worth?' Paul D. Veere says.

'Why,' Little Alfie says, 'he is worth anyway fifty G's to me, because,' he says, 'this is the sum Colonel Winn is giving to the winner of the Kentucky Derby, and there is no doubt whatever that Last Hope will be this winner, especially,' Little Alfie says, 'if it comes up mud.'

'I do not carry any such large sum of money as you mention on my person,' Mr Paul D. Veere says, 'but,' he says, 'if you are willing to trust me, I will give you my IOU for same, just to let me ride your horse to the station. I am once the best amateur steeplechase rider in the Hunts Club,' Mr Paul D. Veere says, 'and if your horse can run at all there is still a chance for me to keep out of jail.'

Well, the chances are Little Alfie will by no means consider extending a loan of credit for fifty G's to Mr Paul D. Veere or any other banker, and especially a banker who is once an amateur steeplechase jock, because if there is one thing Little Alfie does not trust it is an amateur steeplechase jock, and furthermore Little Alfie is somewhat offended because Mr Paul D. Veere seems to think he is running a livery stable.

But Miss Beulah Beauregard is now crying so loud nobody can scarcely hear themselves think, and Little Alfie gets to figuring what she may say to him if he does not rent Last Hope to Mr Paul D. Veere at this time and it comes out later that Last Hope does not happen to win the Kentucky Derby after all. So he finally says all right, and Mr Paul D. Veere at once outs with a little gold pencil and a notebook, and scribbles off a marker for fifty G's to Little Alfie.

And the next thing anybody knows, Little Alfie is leading Last Hope out of the barn and up to the gate with nothing on him but a bridle as Little Alfie does not wish to waste time saddling, and as he is boosting Mr Paul D. Veere on to Last Hope Little Alfie speaks as follows:

'You have three minutes left,' Little Alfie says. 'It is almost a straight course, except for a long turn going into the last quarter. Let this fellow run,' he says. 'You will find plenty of mud all the way, but,' Little Alfie says, 'this is a mud-running fool. In fact,' Little Alfie says, 'you are pretty lucky it comes up mud.'

Then he gives Last Hope a smack on the hip and away goes Last Hope lickity-split through the mud and anybody can see from the way Mr Paul D. Veere is sitting on him that

Mr Paul D. Veere knows what time it is when it comes to riding. In fact, Little Alfie himself says he never sees a better seat anywhere in his life, especially for a guy who is riding bareback.

Well, Little Alfie watches them go down the road in a gob of mud, and it will always be one of the large regrets of Little Alfie's life that he leaves his split-second super in hock in Miami, because he says he is sure Last Hope runs the first quarter through the mud faster than any quarter is ever run before in this world. But of course Little Alfie is more excited than somewhat at this moment, and the chances are he exaggerates Last Hope's speed.

However, there is no doubt that Last Hope goes over the road very rapidly, indeed, as a coloured party who is out squirrel hunting comes along a few minutes afterward and tells Little Alfie that something goes past him on the road so fast he cannot tell exactly what it is, but he states that he is pretty sure it is old Henry Devil himself, because he smells smoke as it passes him, and hears a voice yelling hi-yah. But of course the chances are this voice is nothing but the voice of Mr Paul D. Veere yelling words of encouragement to Last Hope.

It is not until the station-master at Tillinghast, a guy by the name of Asbury Potts, drives over to Miss Beulah Beauregard's ancestral home an hour later that Little Alfie hears that as Last Hope pulls up at the station and Mr Paul D. Veere dismounts with so much mud on him that nobody can tell if he is a plaster cast or what, the horse is gimping as bad as Mr Paul D. Veere himself, and Asbury Potts says there is no doubt Last Hope bows a tendon, or some such, and that if they are able to get him to the races again he will eat his old wool hat.

'But, personally,' Asbury Potts says as he mentions this sad news, 'I do not see what Mr Paul D. Veere's hurry is, at that, to be pushing a horse so hard. He has fifty-seven seconds left by my watch when the Orange Blossom pulls in right on time to the dot,' Asbury Potts says.

Well, at this Little Alfie sits down and starts figuring, and finally he figures that Last Hope runs the mile and a quarter in around 2.03 in the mud, with maybe one hundred and sixty pounds up, for Mr Paul D. Veere is no feather duster, and no horse ever runs a mile and a quarter in the mud in the Kentucky Derby as fast as this, or anywhere else as far as anybody knows, so Little Alfie claims that this is practically flying.

But of course few citizens ever accept Little Alfie's figures as strictly official, because they do not know if Asbury Potts's watch is properly regulated for timing race horses, even though Asbury Potts is 100 per cent right when he says they will never be able to get Last Hope to the races again.

Well, I meet up with Little Alfie one night this summer in Mindy's Restaurant on Broadway, and it is the first time he is observed in these parts in some time, and he seems to be looking very prosperous, indeed, and after we get to cutting up old touches, he tells me the reason for this prosperity.

It seems that after Mr Paul D. Veere returns to New York and puts back in his bank whatever it is that it is advisable for him to put back, or takes out whatever it is that seems best to take out, and gets himself all rounded up so there is no chance of his going to jail, he remembers that there is a slight difference between him and Little Alfie, so what does Mr Paul D. Veere do but sit down and write out a cheque for fifty G's to Little Alfie to take up his IOU, so Little Alfie is nothing out on account of losing the Kentucky Derby, and, in fact, he is stone rich, and I am glad to hear of it, because I always sympathize deeply with him in his bereavement over the loss of Last Hope. Then I ask Little Alfie what he is doing in New York at this time, and he states to me as follows:

'Well,' Little Alfie says, 'I will tell you. The other day,' he says, 'I get to thinking things over, and among other things I get to thinking that after Last Hope wins the Kentucky Derby, he is a sure thing to go on and also win the Maryland Preakness, because,' Little Alfie says, 'the Preakness is a sixteenth of a mile shorter than the Derby, and a horse that can run a mile and a quarter in the mud in around 2.03 with a brick house on his back is bound to make anything that wears hair look silly at a mile and three-sixteenths, especially,' Little Alfie says, 'if it comes up mud.'

'So,' Little Alfie says, 'I am going to call on Mr Paul D. Veere and see if he does not wish to pay me the Preakness stake, too, because,' he says, 'I am building the finest house in South Georgia at Last Hope, which is my stock farm where Last Hope himself is on public exhibition, and I can always use a few bobs here and there.'

'Well, Alfie,' I say, 'this seems to me to be a very fair proposition, indeed, and,' I say, 'I am sure Mr Paul D. Veere 69 will take care of it as soon as it is called to his attention, as there is no doubt you and Last Hope are of great service to Mr Paul D. Veere. By the way, Alfie,' I say, 'whatever becomes of Governor Hicks?'

'Why,' Little Alfie says, 'do you know Governor Hicks turns out to be a terrible disappointment to me as a plough horse? He learns how to sit down from Abimelech, the mule, and nothing will make him stir, not even the same encouragement I give him the day he drops down there third at Hialeah.

'But,' Little Alfie says, 'my ever-loving wife is figuring on using the old Governor as a saddle-horse for our twins, Beulah and Little Alfie, Junior, when they get old enough, although,' he says, 'I tell her the Governor will never be worth a dime in such a way especially,' Little Alfie says, 'if it comes up mud.'

A Very Honourable Guy

Off and on I know Feet Samuels a matter of eight or ten
years, up and down Broadway, and in and out, but I never
have much truck with him because he is a guy I consider no
dice. In fact, he does not mean a thing.

In the first place, Feet Samuels is generally broke, and
there is no percentage in hanging around brokers. The way I
look at it, you are not going to get anything off a guy who has
not got anything. So while I am very sorry for brokers, and
am always willing to hope that they get hold of something, I
do not like to be around them. Long ago an old-timer who
knows what he is talking about says to me:

'My boy,' he says, 'always try to rub up against money, for
if you rub up against money long enough, some of it may rub
off on you.'

So in all the years I am around this town, I always try to
keep in with the high shots and guys who carry these large
coarse banks notes around with them, and I stay away from
small operators and chisellers and brokers. And Feet Samuels
is one of the worst brokers in this town, and has been such as
long as I know him.

He is a big heavy guy with several chins and very funny
feet, which is why he is called Feet. These feet are extra large
feet, even for a big guy, and Dave the Dude says Feet wears
violin-cases for shoes. Of course this is not true, because Feet

cannot get either of his feet in a violin-case, unless it is a case for a very large violin, such as a 'cello.

I see Feet one night in the Hot Box, which is a night club, dancing with a doll by the name of Hortense Hathaway, who is in Georgie White's 'Scandals,' and what is she doing but standing on Feet's feet as if she is on sled runners, and Feet never knows it. He only thinks the old gondolas are a little extra heavy to shove around this night, because Hortense is no invalid. In fact, she is a good rangy welterweight.

She has blonde hair and plenty to say, and her square monicker is Annie O'Brien, and not Hortense Hathaway at all. Furthermore, she comes from Newark, which is in New Jersey, and her papa is a taxi jockey by the name of Skush O'Brien, and a very rough guy, at that, if anybody asks you. But of course the daughter of a taxi jockey is as good as anybody else for Georgie White's 'Scandals' as long as her shape is okay, and nobody ever hears any complaint from the customers about Hortense on this proposition.

She is what is called a show girl, and all she has to do is to walk around and about Georgie White's stage with only a few light bandages on, and everybody considers her very beautiful, especially from the neck down, although personally I never care much for Hortense because she is very fresh to people. I often see her around the night clubs, and when she is in these deadfalls Hortense generally is wearing quite a number of diamond bracelets and fur wraps, and one thing and another, so I judge she is not doing bad for a doll from Newark, New Jersey.

Of course Feet Samuels never knows why so many other

dolls besides Hortense are wishing to dance with him, but gets to thinking maybe it is because he has the old sex appeal, and he is very sore indeed when Henri, the head waiter at the Hot Box, asks him to please stay off the floor except for every tenth dance, because Feet's feet take up so much room when he is on the floor that only two other dancers can work out at the same time, it being a very small floor.

I must tell you more about Feet's feet, because they are very remarkable feet indeed. They go off at different directions under him, very sharp, so if you see Feet standing on a corner it is very difficult to tell which way he is going, because one foot will be headed one way, and the other foot the other way. In fact, guys around Mindy's restaurant often make bets on the proposition as to which way Feet is headed when he is standing still.

What Feet Samuels does for a living is the best he can, which is the same thing many other guys in this town do for a living. He hustles some around the race tracks and crap games and prize fights, picking up a few bobs here and there as a runner for the bookmakers, or scalping bets, or steering suckers, but he is never really in the money in his whole life. He is always owing and always paying off, and I never see him but what he is troubled with the shorts as regards to dough.

The only good thing you can say about Feet Samuels is he is very honourable about his debts, and what he owes he pays when he can. Anybody will tell you this about Feet Samuels, although of course it is only what any hustler such as Feet must do if he wishes to protect his credit and keep in action. Still, you will be surprised how many guys forget to pay.

It is because Feet's word is considered good at all times that he is nearly always able to raise a little dough, even off The Brain, and The Brain is not an easy guy for anybody to raise dough off of. In fact, The Brain is very tough about letting people raise dough off of him.

If anybody gets any dough off of The Brain he wishes to know right away what time they are going to pay it back, with certain interest, and if they say at five-thirty Tuesday morning, they better not make it five-thirty-one Tuesday morning, or The Brain will consider them very unreliable and never let them have any money again. And when a guy loses his credit with The Brain he is in a very tough spot indeed in this town, for The Brain is the only man who always has dough.

Furthermore, some very unusual things often happen to guys who get money off of The Brain and fail to kick it back just when they promise, such as broken noses and sprained ankles and other injuries, for The Brain has people around him who seem to resent guys getting dough off of him and not kicking it back. Still, I know of The Brain letting some very surprising guys have dough, because he has a bug that he is a wonderful judge of guys' characters, and that he is never wrong on them, although I must say that no guy who gets dough off of The Brain is more surprising than Feet Samuels.

The Brain's right name is Armand Rosenthal, and he is

called The Brain because he is so smart. He is well known to one and all in this town as a very large operator in gambling, and one thing and another, and nobody knows how much dough The Brain has, except that he must have plenty, because no matter how much dough is around, The Brain sooner or later gets hold of all of it. Some day I will tell you more about The Brain, but right now I wish to tell you about Feet Samuels.

It comes on a tough winter in New York, what with nearly all hands who have the price going to Miami and Havana and New Orleans, leaving the brokers behind. There is very little action of any kind in town with the high shots gone, and one night I run into Feet Samuels in Mindy's, and he is very sad indeed. He asks me if I happen to have a finnif on me, but of course I am not giving finnifs to guys like Feet Samuels, and finally he offers to compromise with me for a deuce, so I can see things must be very bad with Feet for him to come down from five dollars to two.

'My rent is away overdue for the shovel and broom,' Feet says, 'and I have a hard-hearted landlady who will not listen to reason. She says she will give me the wind if I do not lay something on the line at once. Things are never so bad with me,' Feet says, 'and I am thinking of doing something very desperate.'

I cannot think of anything very desperate for Feet Samuels to do, except maybe go to work, and I know he is not going to do such a thing no matter what happens. In fact, in all the years I am around Broadway I never know any broker to get desperate enough to go to work.

I once hear Dave the Dude offer Feet Samuels a job riding rum between here and Philly at good wages, but Feet turns it down because he claims he cannot stand the open air, and anyway Feet says he hears riding rum is illegal and may land a guy in the pokey. So I know whatever Feet is going to do will be nothing difficult.

'The Brain is still in town,' I say to Feet. 'Why do you not put the lug on him? You stand okay with him.'

'There is the big trouble,' Feet says. 'I owe The Brain a C note already, and I am supposed to pay him back by four o'clock Monday morning, and where I am going to get a hundred dollars I do not know, to say nothing of the other ten I must give him for interest.'

'What are you figuring on doing?' I ask, for it is now a Thursday, and I can see Feet has very little time to get together such a sum.

'I am figuring on scragging myself,' Feet says, very sad. 'What good am I to anybody? I have no family and no friends, and the world is packing enough weight without me. Yes, I think I will scrag myself.'

'It is against the law to commit suicide in this man's town,' I say, 'although what the law can do to a guy who commits suicide I am never able to figure out.'

'I do not care,' Feet says. 'I am sick and tired of it all. I am especially sick and tired of being broke. I never have more than a few quarters to rub together in my pants pocket. Everything I try turns out wrong. The only thing that keeps me from scragging myself at once is the C note I owe The Brain, because I do not wish to have him going around after

I am dead and gone saying I am no good. And the toughest thing of all,' Feet says, 'is I am in love. I am in love with Hortense.'

'Hortense?' I say, very much astonished indeed. 'Why, Hortense is nothing but a big –'

'Stop!' Feet says. 'Stop right here! I will not have her called a big boloney or whatever else big you are going to call her, because I love her. I cannot live without her. In fact,' Feet says, 'I do not wish to live without her.'

'Well,' I say, 'what does Hortense think about you loving her?'

'She does not know it,' Feet says. 'I am ashamed to tell her, because naturally if I tell her I love her, Hortense will expect me to buy her some diamond bracelets, and naturally I cannot do this. But I think she likes me more than somewhat, because she looks at me in a certain way. But,' Feet says, 'there is some other guy who likes her also, and who is buying her diamond bracelets and what goes with them, which makes it very tough on me. I do not know who the guy is, and I do not think Hortense cares for him so much, but naturally any doll must give serious considera- tion to a guy who can buy her diamond bracelets. So I guess there is nothing for me to do but scrag myself.'

Naturally I do not take Feet Samuels serious, and I forget about his troubles at once, because I figure he will wiggle out some way, but the next night he comes into Mindy's all pleasured up, and I figure he must make a scratch somewhere, for he is walking like a man with about sixty-five dollars on him.

But it seems Feet only has an idea, and very few ideas are worth sixty-five dollars.

'I am laying in bed thinking this afternoon,' Feet says, 'and I get to thinking how I can raise enough dough to pay off The Brain, and maybe a few other guys, and my landlady, and leave a few bobs over to help bury me. I am going to sell my body.'

Well, naturally I am somewhat bewildered by this statement, so I ask Feet to explain, and here is his idea: He is going to find some doctor who wishes a dead body and sell his body to this doctor for as much as he can get, his body to be delivered after Feet scrags himself, which is to be within a certain time.

'I understand,' Feet says, 'that these croakers are always looking for bodies to practise on, and that good bodies are not easy to get nowadays.'

'How much do you figure your body is worth?' I ask.

'Well,' Feet says, 'a body as big as mine ought to be worth at least a G.'

'Feet,' I say, 'this all sounds most gruesome to me. Personally I do not know much about such a proposition, but I do not believe if doctors buy bodies at all that they buy them by the pound. And I do not believe you can get a thousand dollars for your body, especially while you are still alive, because how does a doctor know if you will deliver your body to him?'

'Why,' Feet says, very indignant, 'everybody knows I pay what I owe. I can give The Brain for reference, and he will
78 okay me with anybody for keeping my word.'

Well, it seems to me that there is very little sense to what Feet Samuels is talking about, and anyway I figure that maybe he blows his topper, which is what often happens to brokers, so I pay no more attention to him. But on Monday morning, just before four o'clock, I am in Mindy's, and what happens but in walks Feet with a handful of money, looking much pleased.

The Brain is also there at the table where he always sits facing the door so nobody can pop in on him without him seeing them first, because there are many people in this town that The Brain likes to see first if they are coming in where he is. Feet steps up to the table and lays a C note in front of the Brain and also a sawbuck, and The Brain looks up at the clock and smiles and says:

'Okay, Feet, you are on time.'

It is very unusual for The Brain to smile about anything, but afterwards I hear he wins two C's off of Manny Mandelbaum, who bets him Feet will not pay off on time, so The Brain has a smile coming.

'By the way, Feet,' The Brain says, 'some doctor calls me up today and asks me if your word is good, and you may be glad to know I tell him you are one hundred per cent. I put the okay on you because I know you never fail to deliver on a promise. Are you sick, or something?'

'No,' Feet says, 'I am not sick. I just have a little business deal on with the guy. Thanks for the okay.'

Then he comes over to the table where I am sitting, and I can see he still has money left in his duke. Naturally I am anxious to know where he makes the scratch, and by and by he tells me.

'I put over the proposition I am telling you about,' Feet says. 'I sell my body to a doctor over on Park Avenue by the name of Bodeeker, but I do not get a G for it as I expect. It seems bodies are not worth much right now because there are so many on the market, but Doc Bodeeker gives me four C's on thirty days' delivery.

'I never know it is so much trouble selling a body before,' Feet says. 'Three doctors call the cops on me when I proposition them, thinking I am daffy, but Doc Bodeeker is a nice old guy and is glad to do business with me, especially when I give The Brain as reference. Doc Bodeeker says he is looking for a head shaped just like mine for years, because it seems he is a shark on heads. But,' Feet says, 'I got to figure out some way of scragging myself besides jumping out a window, like I plan, because Doc Bodeeker does not wish my head mussed up.'

'Well,' I say, 'this is certainly most ghastly to me and does not sound legitimate. Does The Brain know you sell your body?'

'No,' Feet says, 'Doc Bodeeker only asks him over the phone if my word is good, and does not tell him why he wishes to know, but he is satisfied with The Brain's okay. Now I am going to pay my landlady, and take up a few other markers here and there, and feed myself up good until it is time to leave this bad old world behind.'

But it seems Feet Samuels does not go to pay his landlady right away. Where he goes is to Johnny Crackow's crap game downtown, which is a crap game with a $500 limit where the high shots seldom go, but where there is always some action for a small operator. And as Feet walks into the joint it seems that Big Nig is trying to make four with the dice, and everybody knows that four is a hard point for Big Nig, or anybody else, to make.

So Feet Samuels looks on a while watching Big Nig trying to make four, and a guy by the name of Whitey offers to take two to one for a C note that Big Nig makes this four, which is certainly more confidence than I will ever have in Big Nig. Naturally Feet hauls out a couple of his C notes at once, as anybody must do who has a couple of C notes, and bets Whitey two hundred to a hundred that Big Nig does not make the four. And right away Big Nig outs with a seven, so Feet wins the bet.

Well, to make a long story short, Feet stands there for some time betting guys that other guys will not make four, or whatever it is they are trying to make with the dice, and the first thing anybody knows Feet Samuels is six G's winner, and has the crap game all crippled up. I see him the next night up in the Hot Box, and this big first baseman, Hortense, is with him, sliding around on Feet's feet, and a blind man can see that she has on at least three more diamond bracelets than ever before.

A night or two later I hear of Feet beating Long George McCormack, a high shot from Los Angeles, out of eighteen G's playing a card game that is called low ball, and Feet Samuels has no more licence to beat a guy like Long George playing low ball than I have to lick Jack Dempsey. But when a guy finally gets his rushes in gambling nothing can stop him for a while; and this is the way it is with Feet. Every night you hear of him winning plenty of dough at this or that.

He comes into Mindy's one morning, and naturally I move over to his table at once, because Feet is now in the money and is a guy anybody can associate with freely. I am just about to ask him how things are going with him, although I know they are going pretty good, when in pops a fierce-looking old guy with his face all covered with grey whiskers that stick out every which way, and whose eyes peek out of these whiskers very wild indeed. Feet turns pale as he sees the guy, but nods at him, and the guy nods back and goes out.

'Who is the Whiskers?' I ask Feet. 'He is in here the other morning looking around, and he makes people very nervous because nobody can figure who he is or what his dodge may be.'

'It is old Doc Bodeeker,' Feet says. 'He is around checking up on me to make sure I am still in town. Say, I am in a very hot spot one way and another.'

'What are you worrying about?' I ask. 'You got plenty of dough and about two weeks left to enjoy yourself before this Doc Bodeeker forecloses on you.'

'I know,' Feet says, very sad. 'But now I get this dough things do not look as tough to me as formerly, and I am very sorry I make the deal with the doctor. Especially,' Feet says, 'on account of Hortense.'

'What about Hortense?' I ask.

'I think she is commencing to love me since I am able to buy her more diamond bracelets than the other guy,' Feet says. 'If it is not for this thing hanging over me, I will ask her to marry me, and maybe she will do it, at that.'

'Well, then,' I say, 'why do you not go to old Whiskers and pay him his dough back, and tell him you change your mind about selling your body, although of course if it is not for Whiskers's buying your body you will not have all this dough.'

'I do go to him,' Feet says, and I can see there are big tears in his eyes. 'But he says he will not cancel the deal. He says he will not take the money back; what he wants is my body, because I have such a funny-shaped head. I offer him four times what he pays me, but he will not take it. He says my body must be delivered to him promptly on March first.'

'Does Hortense know about this deal?' I ask.

'Oh, no, no!' Feet says. 'And I will never tell her, because she will think I am crazy, and Hortense does not care for crazy guys. In fact, she is always complaining about the other guy who buys her the diamond bracelets, claiming he is a little crazy, and if she thinks I am the same way the chances are she will give me the breeze.'

Now this is a situation, indeed, but what to do about it I do not know. I put the proposition up to a lawyer friend of mine the next day, and he says he does not believe the deal will hold good in court, but of course I know Feet Samuels does not wish to go to court, because the last time Feet goes to court he is held as a material witness and is in the Tombs ten days.

The lawyer says Feet can run away, but personally I consider this a very dishonourable idea after The Brain putting the okay on Feet with old Doc Bodeeker, and anyway I can see Feet is not going to do such a thing as long as Hortense is around. I can see that one hair of her head is stronger than the Atlantic cable with Feet Samuels.

A week slides by, and I do not see so much of Feet, but I hear of him murdering crap games and short card players, and winning plenty, and also going around the night clubs with Hortense, who finally has so many bracelets there is no more room on her arms, and she puts a few of them on her ankles, which are not bad ankles to look at, at that, with or without bracelets.

Then goes another week, and it just happens I am standing in front of Mindy's about four-thirty one morning and thinking that Feet's time must be up and wondering how he makes out with old Doc Bodeeker, when all of a sudden I hear a ploppity-plop coming up Broadway, and what do I see but Feet Samuels running so fast he is passing taxis that are going thirty-five miles an hour like they are standing still. He is certainly stepping along.

There are no traffic lights and not much traffic at such an hour in the morning, and Feet passes me in a terrible hurry. And about twenty yards behind him comes an old guy with grey whiskers, and I can see it is nobody but Doc Bodeeker. What is more, he has a big long knife in one hand, and he seems to be reaching for Feet at every jump with the knife.

Well, this seems to me a most surprising spectacle, and I follow them to see what comes of it, because I can see at once that Doc Bodeeker is trying to collect Feet's body himself. But I am not much of a runner, and they are out of my sight in no time, and only that I am able to follow them by ear through Feet's feet going ploppity-plop I will never trail them.

They turn east into Fifty-fourth Street off Broadway, and when I finally reach the corner I see a crowd halfway down the block in front of the Hot Box, and I know this crowd has something to do with Feet and Doc Bodeeker even before I get to the door to find that Feet goes on in while Doc Bodeeker is arguing with Soldier Sweeney, the door man, because as Feet passes the Soldier he tells the Soldier not to let the guy who is chasing him in. And the Soldier, being a good friend of Feet's, is standing the doc off.

Well, it seems that Hortense is in the Hot Box waiting for Feet, and naturally she is much surprised to see him come in all out of breath, and so is everybody else in the joint, including Henri, the head waiter, who afterwards tells me what comes off there, because you see I am out in front.

'A crazy man is chasing me with a butcher knife,' Feet says to Hortense. 'If he gets inside I am a goner. He is down at the door trying to get in.'

Now I will say one thing for Hortense, and this is she has plenty of nerve, but of course you will expect a daughter of Skush O'Brien to have plenty of nerve. Nobody ever has more moxie than Skush. Henri, the head waiter, tells me that Hortense does not get excited, but says she will just have a little peek at the guy who is chasing Feet.

The Hot Box is over a garage, and the kitchen windows look down into Fifty-fourth Street, and while Doc Bodeeker is arguing with Soldier Sweeney, I hear a window lift, and who looks out but Hortense. She takes one squint and yanks her head in quick, and Henri tells me afterwards she shrieks:

'My Lord, Feet! This is the same daffy old guy who sends me all the bracelets, and who wishes to marry me!'

'And he is the guy I sell my body to,' Feet says, and then he tells Hortense the story of his deal with Doc Bodeeker.

'It is all for you, Horty,' Feet says, although of course this is nothing but a big lie, because it is all for The Brain in the beginning. 'I love you, and I only wish to get a little dough to show you a good time before I die. If it is not for this deal I will ask you to be my ever-loving wife.'

Well, what happens but Hortense plunges right into Feet's arms, and gives him a big kiss on his ugly mush, and says to him like this:

'I love you too, Feet, because nobody ever makes such a sacrifice as to hock their body for me. Never mind the deal. I will marry you at once, only we must first get rid of this daffy old guy downstairs.'

Then Hortense peeks out of the window again and hollers down at old Doc Bodeeker. 'Go away,' she says. 'Go away, or I will chuck a moth in your whiskers, you old fool.'

But the sight of her only seems to make old Doc Bodeeker a little wilder than somewhat, and he starts struggling with Soldier Sweeney very ferocious, so the Soldier takes the knife away from the doc and throws it away before somebody gets hurt with it.

Now it seems Hortense looks around the kitchen for something to chuck out the window at old Doc Bodeeker, and all she sees is a nice new ham which the chef just lays out on the table to slice up for ham sandwiches. This ham is a very large ham, such as will last the Hot Box a month, for they slice the ham in their ham sandwiches very, very thin up at the Hot Box. Anyway, Hortense grabs up the ham and runs to the window with it and gives it a heave without even stopping to take aim.

Well, this ham hits the poor old Doc Bodeeker kerbowie smack dab on the noggin. The doc does not fall down, but he commences staggering around with his legs bending under him like he is drunk.

I wish to help him, because I feel sorry for a guy in such a spot as this, and what is more I consider it a dirty trick for a doll such as Hortense to slug anybody with a ham.

Well, I take charge of the old doc and lead him back down Broadway and into Mindy's, where I set him down and get him a cup of coffee and a Bismarck herring to revive him, while quite a number of citizens gather about him very sympathetic.

'My friends,' the old doc says finally, looking around, 'you see in me a broken-hearted man. I am not a crack-pot, although of course my relatives may give you an argument on this proposition. I am in love with Hortense. I am in love with her from the night I first see her playing the part of a sunflower in "Scandals". I wish to marry her, as I am a widower of long standing, but somehow the idea of me marrying anybody never appeals to my sons and daughters.

'In fact,' the doc says, dropping his voice to a whisper, 'sometimes they even talk of locking me up when I wish to marry somebody. So naturally I never tell them about Hortense, because I fear they may try to discourage me. But I am deeply in love with her and send her many beautiful presents, although I am not able to see her often on account of my relatives. Then I find out Hortense is carrying on with this Feet Samuels.

'I am desperately jealous,' the doc says, 'but I do not know what to do. Finally Fate sends this Feet to me offering to sell his body. Of course, I am not practising for years, but I keep an office on Park Avenue just for old times' sake, and it is to this office he comes. At first I think he is crazy, but he refers me to Mr Armand Rosenthal, the big sporting man, who assures me that Feet Samuels is all right.

'The idea strikes me that if I make a deal with Feet Samuels for his body as he proposes, he will wait until the time comes to pay his obligation and run away, and,' the doc says, 'I will never be troubled by his rivalry for the affections of Hortense again. But he does not depart. I do not reckon on the holding power of love.

'Finally in a jealous frenzy I take after him with a knife, figuring to scare him out of town. But it is too late. I can see now Hortense loves him in return, or she will not drop a scuttle of coal on me in his defence as she does.

'Yes, gentlemen,' the old doc says, 'I am broken-hearted. I also seem to have a large lump on my head. Besides, Hortense has all my presents, and Feet Samuels has my money, so I get the worst of it all around. I only hope and trust that my daughter Eloise, who is Mrs Sidney Simmons Bragdon, does not hear of this, or she may be as mad as she is the time I wish to marry the beautiful cigarette girl in Jimmy Kelley's.'

Here Doc Bodeeker seems all busted up by his feelings and starts to shed tears, and everybody is feeling very sorry for him indeed, when up steps The Brain, who is taking everything in.

'Do not worry about your presents and your dough,' The Brain says. 'I will make everything good, because I am the guy who okays Feet Samuels with you. I am wrong on a guy for the first time in my life, and I must pay, but Feet Samuels will be very, very sorry when I find him. Of course, I do not figure on a doll in the case, and this always makes quite a difference, so I am really not a hundred per cent. wrong on the guy, at that.

'But,' The Brain says, in a very loud voice so everybody can hear, 'Feet Samuels is nothing but a dirty welsher for not turning in his body to you as per agreement, and as long as he lives he will never get another dollar or another okay off of me, or anybody I know. His credit is ruined for ever on Broadway.'

But I judge that Feet and Hortense do not care. The last time I hear of them they are away over in New Jersey where not even The Brain's guys dare to bother them on account of Skush O'Brien, and I understand they are raising chickens and children right and left, and that all of Hortense's bracelets are now in Newark municipal bonds, which I am told are not bad bonds, at that.

PENGUIN 60s

MARTIN AMIS · *God's Dice*

HANS CHRISTIAN ANDERSEN · *The Emperor's New Clothes*

MARCUS AURELIUS · *Meditations*

JAMES BALDWIN · *Sonny's Blues*

AMBROSE BIERCE · *An Occurrence at Owl Creek Bridge*

DIRK BOGARDE · *From Le Pigeonnier*

WILLIAM BOYD · *Killing Lizards*

POPPY Z. BRITE · *His Mouth will Taste of Wormwood*

ITALO CALVINO · *Ten Italian Folktales*

ALBERT CAMUS · *Summer*

TRUMAN CAPOTE · *First and Last*

RAYMOND CHANDLER · *Goldfish*

ANTON CHEKHOV · *The Black Monk*

ROALD DAHL · *Lamb to the Slaughter*

ELIZABETH DAVID · *I'll be with You in the Squeezing of a Lemon*

N. J. DAWOOD (TRANS.) · *The Seven Voyages of Sindbad the Sailor*

ISAK DINESEN · *The Dreaming Child*

SIR ARTHUR CONAN DOYLE · *The Man with the Twisted Lip*

DICK FRANCIS · *Racing Classics*

SIGMUND FREUD · *Five Lectures on Psycho-Analysis*

KAHLIL GIBRAN · *Prophet, Madman, Wanderer*

STEPHEN JAY GOULD · *Adam's Navel*

ALASDAIR GRAY · *Five Letters from an Eastern Empire*

GRAHAM GREENE · *Under the Garden*

JAMES HERRIOT · *Seven Yorkshire Tales*

PATRICIA HIGHSMITH · *Little Tales of Misogyny*

M. R. JAMES AND R. L. STEVENSON · *The Haunted Dolls' House*

RUDYARD KIPLING · *Baa Baa, Black Sheep*

PENELOPE LIVELY · *A Long Night at Abu Simbel*

KATHERINE MANSFIELD · *The Escape*

READ MORE IN PENGUIN

For complete information about books available from Penguin and how to order them, please write to us at the appropriate address below. Please note that for copyright reasons the selection of books varies from country to country.

IN THE UNITED KINGDOM: Please write to *Dept. JC, Penguin Books Ltd, FREEPOST, West Drayton, Middlesex UB7 OBR.*
If you have any difficulty in obtaining a title, please send your order with the correct money, plus ten per cent for postage and packaging, to *PO Box No. 11, West Drayton, Middlesex UB7 OBR.*

IN THE UNITED STATES: Please write to *Consumer Sales, Penguin USA, P.O. Box 999, Dept. 17109, Bergenfield, New Jersey 07621-0120.* VISA and MasterCard holders call 1-800-253-6476 to order all Penguin titles.

IN CANADA: Please write to *Penguin Books Canada Ltd, 10 Alcorn Avenue, Suite 300, Toronto, Ontario M4V 3B2.*

IN AUSTRALIA: Please write to *Penguin Books Australia Ltd, P.O. Box 257, Ringwood, Victoria 3134.*

IN NEW ZEALAND: Please write to *Penguin Books (NZ) Ltd, Private Bag 102902, North Shore Mail Centre, Auckland 10.*

IN INDIA: Please write to *Penguin Books India Pvt Ltd, 706 Eros Apartments, 56 Nehru Place, New Delhi 110 019.*

IN THE NETHERLANDS: Please write to *Penguin Books Netherlands bv, Postbus 3507, NL-1001 AH Amsterdam.*

IN GERMANY: Please write to *Penguin Books Deutschland GmbH, Metzlerstrasse 26, 60594 Frankfurt am Main.*

IN SPAIN: Please write to *Penguin Books S. A., Bravo Murillo 19, 1o B, 28015 Madrid.*

IN ITALY: Please write to *Penguin Italia s.r.l., Via Felice Casati 20, I-20124 Milano.*

IN FRANCE: Please write to *Penguin France S. A., 17 rue Lejeune, F-31000 Toulouse.*

IN JAPAN: Please write to *Penguin Books Japan, Ishikiribashi Building, 2-5-4, Suido, Bunkyo-ku, Tokyo 112.*

IN GREECE: Please write to *Penguin Hellas Ltd, Dimocritou 3, GR-106 71 Athens.*

IN SOUTH AFRICA: Please write to *Longman Penguin Southern Africa (Pty) Ltd, Private Bag X08, Bertsham 2013.*

MACNEILL, A.

DOUBLE-BLIND

596452

(797)

F